H. P. Lovecraft

H. P. Lovecraft

Midnight Studies

Jan B. W. Pedersen

PETER LANG
Oxford - Berlin - Bruxelles - Chennai - Lausanne - New York

Bibliographic information published by the Deutsche Nationalbibliothek. The German National Library lists this publication in the German National Bibliography; detailed bibliographic data is available on the Internet at http://dnb.d-nb.de.

A catalogue record for this book is available from the British Library.

Library of Congress Cataloging-in-Publication Data

Names: Pedersen, Jan B. W., author. | Joshi, S. T., 1958- writer of foreword.
Title: H. P. Lovecraft: midnight studies / Jan B. W. Pedersen.
Description: Oxford; New York: Peter Lang, [2024] | Includes bibliographical references and index.
Identifiers: LCCN 2024010093 (print) | LCCN 2024010094 (ebook) | ISBN 9781803743073 (hardback) | ISBN 9781803743134 (ebook) | ISBN 9781803743141 (epub)
Subjects: LCSH: Lovecraft, H. P. (Howard Phillips), 1890-1937--Criticism and interpretation. | Wonder in literature. | Romanticism. | American literature--19th century--History and criticism. | Authors, American--20th century--Biography.
Classification: LCC PS3523.O833 Z834 2024 (print) | LCC PS3523.O833 (ebook) | DDC 813.5/2--dc23/eng/20240521
LC record available at https://lccn.loc.gov/2024010093
LC ebook record available at https://lccn.loc.gov/2024010094

Cover image: Harry Evans, *Dunsanian*, 2023. Courtesy of Harry Evans.
Cover design by Peter Lang Group AG

ISBN 978-1-80374-307-3 (print)
ISBN 978-1-80374-313-4 (ePDF)
ISBN 978-1-80374-314-1 (ePub)
DOI 10.3726/b21241

Published by Peter Lang Ltd, Oxford, United Kingdom
info@peterlang.com – www.peterlang.com

For Ayako and Mai

Contents

Figures

S. T. JOSHI

Foreword

That H. P. Lovecraft (1890–1937) has become a worldwide literary and cultural phenomenon would have been a surprise to no one more than to Lovecraft himself. Having lived most of his life in poverty, and having seen not a single book of his stories published in his lifetime, Lovecraft would be amazed at the dissemination of his work not only in countless English-language editions but also in translations into more than thirty languages, including all the major languages of Europe.

It is one thing, however, to attain celebrity as an icon of popular culture, as Lovecraft has done, if we look at the numerous adaptations of his work in film, television, comic books and over media; it is an altogether different thing for him to have achieved the level of critical acclaim and scholarly attention that he has received, especially in the last half-century. American scholars may have taken the lead in interpreting his work and in revealing its philosophical and aesthetic depth, but European scholars have not been far behind.

The French, more responsive to expressions of *le fantastique* than their Anglo-American counterparts, embraced Lovecraft as early as the 1950s, and critics from Jean Cocteau to Michel Houellebecq have sung his praises. Maurice Lévy wrote a dissertation on Lovecraft for the Sorbonne in 1969; it was published as a monograph, *Lovecraft ou du fantastique* (1972). Scholarly treatments of Lovecraft's work have appeared in German (Theka Zachrau's *Mytghos und Phantastik: Funktion und Struktur der Cthulhu-Mythologie in den phantastischen Erzählungen H. P. Lovecrafts*, 1986), Spanish (Juan-Jacobo Bajarlia's *H. P. Lovecraft: El horror sobrenatural*, 1996), Swedish (Mattias Fyhr's *Dod men drömmande: H. P. Lovecraft och den magiska modernismen,* 2006), Italian (Massimo Di Giovanni's *Il concetto di trasfigurazione in H. P. Lovecraft*, 2006) and other languages. The Finnish scholar Timo Airaksinen has written a challenging treatise in English, *The Philosophy of H. P. Lovecraft* (1999).

Now, the Danish scholar Jan B. W. Pedersen, in *H. P. Lovecraft: Midnight Studies*, adds significantly to the already substantial body of Lovecraft criticism and scholarship by presenting a daring thesis – that Lovecraft was a Romantic, in spite of his avowed devotion to classical antiquity and the classicising writers of eighteenth-century England. Pedersen presents compelling evidence for this thesis while also illuminating Lovecraft's life and work in other ways. He has drawn upon the massive body of Lovecraft's surviving letters, which exist in a total of nearly five million words and are remarkably illuminating as to the author's life, his literary work and his outlook on life.

The genre of weird fiction, to which Lovecraft devoted much of his literary career, may perhaps be seen as intrinsically an expression of Romantic aesthetics, given that it was born in the late eighteenth century, when the Gothic novel emerged as a reaction to the stifling classicism of the earlier phase of the century. And yet, Lovecraft, while philosophically inclined towards classicism in terms of his atheism and his devotion to science, found in weird fiction a means of fusing classicism and Romanticism in a dynamic manner.

Lovecraft was one of the most well-read authors of weird fiction, and Pedersen studies one of the author's most significant influences, the Anglo-Irish writer Lord Dunsany, in a chapter of this book. Both writers exhibit an incipient Romanticism that is not obvious on the surface of their work.

Pedersen has also focused on lesser-known bodies of Lovecraft's work, such as his poetry. His chapter on 'Lovecraft's Garden' studies a seemingly slight poem, 'A Garden,' seeing it as a window through which the author's Romantic tendencies can be detected. Lovecraft's lifelong teetotalism may also seem remote from the main thesis of this book, but Pedersen highlights the relevance of this stance to Lovecraft's overall social philosophy.

Jan B. W. Pedersen, in a series of essays that reveal an acute sensitivity to the nuances of Lovecraft's literary expression in both prose and poetry, has made a vital contribution to the study of this enigmatic author, whose work continues to engage and stimulate us more than a century after it was written.

Acknowledgements

In his moral epistle to Lucilius entitled *On Benefits* the Roman Stoic philosopher Seneca writes that 'Anyone who receives a benefit more gladly than he repays it is mistaken.[1] There is wisdom in such words and in what follows I shall happily acknowledge those excellent folk whose wisdom, knowledge and skills I have benefited from while researching and putting together *H. P. Lovecraft: Midnight Studies.*

First and foremost, I would like to express my indebtedness to Lovecraft scholar par excellence S. T. Joshi for encouraging the book at hand and for kindly providing the foreword.

I have also profited from many a philosophical discussion with Dr Hans Fink, Professor Emeritus of philosophy at Aarhus University and specifically so on the topic of 'reality' which plays a significant part in the final chapter of the book.

Thanks also to Dr Anders Schinkel, Associate Professor at Vrije University for his enduring encouragement, many kind words and for inviting me to speak on Lovecraft and wonder at the 2019 international conference *Wonder, Education, and Human Flourishing*. In this regard I should like to express yet again my gratitude to the many academics who attended my talk. Your genuine interest and perceptive questions were challenging and highly motivating.

The present volume incorporates various artwork, and I am chiefly indebted to artists extraordinaire Lez Edwards and Harry Evans for their highly atmospheric contributions.

I am likewise grateful to Dr Eri Mountbatten-O'Malley, Senior Lecturer at Bath Spa University and to my old friend Claus Simonsen for numerous joyful conversations and moral support.

Thanks also to my brothers Lars and Kim Pedersen for their ongoing backing and encouragement.

1 Seneca, 'On Benefits', in *Epistles 66–92*, Richard M. Cummere, trans., Loeb Classical Library (Cambridge, MA: Harvard University Press), 231.

H. P. Lovecraft: Midnight Studies would not have taken its present form without the assistance of my excellent friend and fellow Lovecraftian Geoff Byers whose careful language corrections and critique helped me steer clear of many embarrassments.

I am also grateful to my editor Dr Laurel Plapp at Peter Lang Oxford and two anonymous reviewers for their kind professionalism and help.

Finally, I would like to extend my gratitude to my wife Dr Ayako Wakatsuki Pedersen for encouraging me to work on Lovecraft in the first place and to my daughter Mai for supplying me with a multitude of Cthulhu cakes and depictions of Shoggoths over the years. As a result of your efforts, I am a better Lovecraftian (or cultist) today. *Iä! R'lyeh! Cthulhu fhtagn! Iä! Iä!*

Earlier versions of Chapters 1–5, and an excerpt from the Introduction, appear in *Lovecraft Annual* No. 11, 12, 13 and 16, published between 2017 and 2022, and in the 2020 anthology *Wonder, Education, and Human Flourishing: Theoretical, Empirical, and Practical Perspectives*, edited by Anders Schinkel. These earlier versions are used by permission of Derrick Hussey, Hippocampus Press (<www.hippocampuspress.com>) and Dr Anders Schinkel, VU University Press (<www.vuuniversitypress.com>). Without the support of these fine gentlemen the present volume would have remained inanimate.

Jan B. W. Pedersen
Copenhagen, Denmark
August 2023

Introduction

H. P. Lovecraft: Midnight Studies introduces the notion that the American twentieth-century weird fiction author Howard Phillips Lovecraft at heart was a Romantic. It is a body of work primarily for Lovecraft scholars and enthusiasts but students of gothic and weird fiction might also find it useful and illuminating.

In his sixteenth-century political treatise *De Principatibus*, the Florentine philosopher Niccolò Machiavelli writes: 'There is nothing more difficult to take in hand, more perilous to conduct, or more uncertain in its success, than to take the lead in the introduction of a new order of things.'[1] In relation to *H. P. Lovecraft: Midnight Studies* such wisdom is to some extent fitting because it represents a new way of thinking about Lovecraft. To elaborate I should first of all point out that the work that went into the book has been difficult to conduct because it has taken place primarily during the small hours of the morning, when the world takes on a different hue and a fear partly justified creeps up on you – a fear that, in part, is linked to the soul of these weird hours and partly animated by the circumstances I found myself in at the time. The whole matter began, so far as I am concerned, one late afternoon in the autumn of 2016, when my wife Ayako suggested that I should write an article on Lovecraft. I had recently finished my doctorate specialising in the philosophy of 'wonder' and 'human flourishing' and was struggling to find an academic job in the UK that would allow me to continue my research. It was a troublesome period with little income, complemented by an ever-growing desperation, and to compensate I had sought refuge in Lovecraft's fiction and biography. At first, I was sceptical about her suggestion because I was not an expert on Lovecraft, but I soon found myself in the process of outlining the article 'On Lovecraft's Lifelong Relationship with Wonder' that appears as the first

1 Niccolò Machiavelli, *The Prince*, W. K. Marriot, trans. (Project Gutenberg, 1998), chapter 6.

chapter in the present volume. It was a highly nourishing process that fused scholarly forte with what inevitably became a deep fascination with the life and times of the gentleman of Providence. The article was published in 2017 and by then my family and I had moved to Denmark, where I had secured employment and much-needed income as a college lecturer. Unfortunately, the position did not encourage my Lovecraft studies, but I continued the habit of working on Lovecraft in the small hours of the morning, and over the course of the subsequent six years I managed to further my studies in the form of more publications and occasional conference and convention talks, thus laying the groundwork for the book at hand.

Secondly, I should point out that introducing Lovecraft as a Romantic is perilous because being Romantic is suggestive of a proposition seemingly at odds with Lovecraft's well-known scientific and materialist inclinations. From an early age Lovecraft was fascinated by astronomy, chemistry and meteorology and he produced several smaller treatises on astronomical matters of which some are now curated by the famous John Hay Library at Brown University.[2] With regard to materialism, we find his commitment firmly stated in the 1919 essay 'Idealism and Materialism' and in his 1926 letter to Walter J. Coates.[3] In the same vein one might take issue with the idea of Lovecraft being a Romantic because of his racism manifested in works such as the poem 'On the Creation of Niggers' written in 1912; the short story 'The Horror of Red Hook' published in 1927; and his letter to Elizabeth Toldridge dated 10 March 1930.[4] Naturally this rests on how

2 S. T. Joshi, ed., '"Introduction" & "Note on This Edition"' in *Collected Essays: Volume 3: Science* (New York: Hippocampus Press, 2005), 9–13 and August Derleth & Donald Wandrei, eds, *H. P. Lovecraft Selected Letters II* (Sauk City, WI: Arkham House Publishers, 1968), 211, 41. See also Fred S. Lubnow's illuminating 'The Lovecraftian Solar System', in S. T. Joshi, ed., *Lovecraft Annual No. 13* (New York: Hippocampus Press, 2019), 3–26 and Horace A. Smith's excellent article 'Lovecraft Seeks the Garden of Eratosthenes' also in S. T. Joshi, ed., *Lovecraft Annual No. 13* (New York: Hippocampus Press, 2019), 153–176.

3 See S. T. Joshi, ed., 'Idealism and Materialism—A Reflection', in *Collected Essays Volume 5: Philosophy, Autobiography & Miscellany* (New York: Hippocampus Press, 2006), 38–45.

4 See S. T. Joshi, ed., 'On the Creation of Niggers', in *The Ancient Track: The Complete Poetical Works of H. P. Lovecraft* (New York: Hippocampus Press, 2013), 389;

one views Romanticism but to think openness towards what is foreign inherent to Romanticism has some merit. Just think of English Romantic poet John Keats' 1817 poem 'Happy is England'. The poem reveals Keats' desire for Italian beauties of a deeper glance, his longing not only to hear their singing but also to float with them about the summer waters.[5] One can also look to the Romantic Thomas Edward Lawrence better known as Lawrence of Arabia for guidance because according to biographer Dick Benson-Gyles, Lawrence loved Farida al Akle – the lady who taught him Arabic in Lebanon.[6] Regardless I would like to make it quite clear that the present book offers no refutations of Lovecraft's fondness of science and proclivity towards materialism, nor does it propose any explanation or apology for his racism. It merely presents evidence in favour of another Lovecraft – a Lovecraft endowed with longings and sensibilities that thus far has remained unsung in Lovecraft scholarship.

Thirdly, arguing that Lovecraft at heart was a Romantic is precarious business because it is difficult to define what Romanticism is and without a clear definition the project would seem futile and impotent. Now, to be clear, *H. P. Lovecraft: Midnight Studies* presents no final or exact definition of Romanticism but the reader will gain insight into what the distinguished and perceptive philosopher Bertrand Russell described as 'a way of feeling' or what people in France during the eighteenth century labelled 'la sensibilité', referring to a certain proneness to emotion or sympathy which must be direct, violent and uninformed by thought in order to be fully Romantic.[7] The reader will also gain insight into Romanticism understood as a movement which the eminent historian of ideas Isaiah Berlin described as dangerous, confusing and the force behind 'a gigantic

---

Leslie S. Klinger, ed., 'The Horror at Red Hook', in *The New Annotated H. P. Lovecraft: Beyond Arkham* (New York: Liveright Publishing Corporation, 2019), 249–276 and August Derleth & Donald Wandrei, eds, *H. P. Lovecraft Selected Letters III* (Sauk City, WI: Arkham House Publishers, 1971), 120.

5 See John Keats, 'Happy Is England', in *The Complete Poems of John Keats*, John Barnard, ed. (London: Penguin Books, 1988).

6 See Dick Benson-Gyles, *The Boy in the Mask: The Hidden World of Lawrence of Arabia* (Dublin: The Lilliput Press, 2016).

7 Bertrand Russell, *History of Western Philosophy* (London: Routledge, 2009), 545.

and radical transformation, after which nothing was ever the same'.[8] In this sense we might say that Romanticism equals rebellion against the established and can be seen as an intellectual showdown that ultimately brings something new to the table. What is this 'new' then? Well, the 'new' is perhaps not new at all but as old as humankind itself. In reference to philosopher Friedrich Schlegel Berlin explains that there is in all of us a 'terrible unsatisfied desire to soar into infinity, a feverish longing to break through the narrow bonds of individuality'.[9] A possible rendition of this somewhat cryptic explanation is that the Romantic person harbours a particular emotional drive that will not be denied. A form of craving that is as much intellectual as it is felt – an urge unlike any other that aims at two goals (1) to comprehend the world as it is and not merely as it appears to be and (2) to merge with it in such a way that individuality and isolation forevermore will be a thing of the past. Now the intensity of this drive is important to understand because it plays to its undeniability. The drive, urge or feeling has the air of eros about it and like the immortal souls in Plato's dialogue *Phaedrus* the Romantics metaphorically speaking entertain a burning desire to stand upon the outside of heaven where the revolution of the spheres carries them around so they may behold things beyond.[10]

Having said that Romanticism also refers to what French writer Ferdinand Brunetière explains as literary egoism, individuality at the expense of a larger world, and the opposite of self-transcendence.[11] Like in Schlegel's explanation what is at stake here is not entirely clear but I take it to mean that Romanticism or to be more precise Romantic writing can also be about utter self-assertion – an expression of a certain egomania that promotes a moral outlook centring not so much on the bettering of oneself in relation to others but on self-interest only.

Obviously understanding Romanticism is challenging because it is in a sense a melting pot filled with opposites and thus whatever definition of

8 See Isaiah Berlin, *The Roots of Romanticism*, Henry Hardy, ed. (Princeton, NJ: Princeton University Press, 2001), 1.

9 Ibid., 15.

10 See Platon, 'Phaidros' (Phaedo), in *Platon II samlede værker*, Jørgen Mejer & Chr. Gorm Tortzen, eds (Copenhagen: Gyldendal, 2010), 420 (247b).

11 See Berlin, *The Roots of Romanticism*,, 15.

Romanticism one may encounter or indeed produce is as likely to go unchallenged as it is to be challenged. On the outset this may seem somewhat strange, but it is nevertheless apt because Romanticism as Berlin intensely informed the amused audience during his March/April 1965 A. W. Mellon Lectures on Romanticism at the National Gallery of Art in Washington is:

> The strange, the exotic, the grotesque, the mysterious, the supernatural, ruins, moonlight, enchanted castles, hunting horns, elves, giants, griffins, falling water, the old mill on the Floss, darkness, and the powers of darkness, phantoms, vampires, nameless terror, the irrational, the unutterable. Also it is the familiar, the sense of one's unique tradition, joy in the smiling aspects of everyday nature, and the accustomed sights and sounds of contented, simple, rural folk – the sane and happy wisdom of rosy-cheeked sons of the soil. It is the ancient, the historic, it is Gothic cathedrals, mists of antiquity, ancient roots and the old order with its unanalysable qualities, its profound but inexpressible loyalties, the impalpable, the imponderable. Also it is the pursuit of novelty, revolutionary change, concern with the fleeting present, desire to live in the moment, rejection of knowledge, past and future, the pastoral idyll of happy ignorance, joy in the passing instant, a sense of timelessness. It is nostalgia, it is reverie, it is intoxicating dreams, it is sweet melancholy and bitter melancholy, solitude, the sufferings of exile, the sense of alienation, roaming in remote places, especially the East, and in remote times, especially in the Middle Ages [...] It is beauty and ugliness. It is art for the art's sake, and art as an instrument of social salvation. It is strength and weakness, individualism and collectivism, purity and corruption, revolution and reaction, peace and war, love of life and love of death.[12]

Now as daunting if not ludicrous as this may seem it is against this very backdrop of confusion that I intend to present to you the Lovecraft that I, after several years of study, have come to see and enjoy.

Fourthly, the book may for some academics be difficult to accept because it does not offer a huge amount of engagement with other Lovecraft scholars and could potentially come across as a body of work conducted in a vacuum. This is not the case, but because the central point made throughout *H. P. Lovecraft: Midnight Studies* is original and because no other work to the best of my knowledge deals directly with Lovecraft and Romanticism references to other academic works on Lovecraft are minimal.

12 See Ibid.,, 16–17.

Having said that, I am deeply indebted to many a Lovecraftian scholar including S. T. Joshi and his colossal contribution to Lovecraft scholarship. I am particularly thankful for the 1980 anthology *H. P. Lovecraft: Four Decades of Criticism*; his 2003 collection of essays: *Primal Sources: Essays on H. P. Lovecraft* and *An H. P. Lovecraft Encyclopedia* which he made together with David E. Schultz.[13] Likewise, I am grateful to Eugene Thacker and his work on 'life' and how it poses a problem for philosophy, together with his *Horror of Philosophy* trilogy, centring on the relationship between philosophy and the horror genre. Published between 2011 and 2015 they all engage with H. P. Lovecraft and are thoroughly fascinating and informative.[14] Philip Smith's 2011 essay 'Re-visioning Romantic-Era Gothicism: An Introduction to Key Works and Themes in the Study of H. P. Lovecraft' is also worth mentioning as it establishes Lovecraft's place in Gothic literary cannon and the same goes for Graham Harman's *Weird Realism: Lovecraft and Philosophy* from 2012 because it explores the impact of Lovecraft on philosophy in general and the Speculative Realist movement in particular.[15] Additionally I have enjoyed the 2013 anthology *New Critical Essays on H. P. Lovecraft* edited by David Simmons and Bobby Derie's pioneering *Sex and The Cthulhu Mythos* from 2014 which focuses on the topic of sex in relation to Lovecraft and his oeuvre in a most insightful way.[16] Equally I have over the years benefitted from numerous astute contributions to the periodical *Lovecraft Annual* but especially Dennis Quinn's informative 'Endless Bacchanal: Rome, Livy, and Lovecraft's Cthulhu Cult'; James

13 S. T. Joshi, ed., *H. P. Lovecraft: Four Decades of Criticism* (Athens, OH: Ohio University Press, 1980); S. T. Joshi, *Primal Sources: Essays on H. P. Lovecraft* (New York: Hippocampus Press, 2003) and S. T. Joshi & David E. Schultz, *An H. P. Lovecraft Encyclopedia* (New York: Hippocampus Press, 2001).

14 Eugene Thacker, *After Life* (Chicago: The University of Chicago Press, 2010) and *Horror of Philosophy*, vols 1–3 (Winchester: Zero Books, 2010/2015).

15 See Philip Smith, Re-visioning Romantic-Era Gothicism: An Introduction to Key Works and Themes in the Study of H. P. Lovecraft', *Literature Compass* 8/11 (2011), 830–839 & Graham Harman, *Weird Realism: Lovecraft and Philosophy* (Winchester: Zero Books, 2012).

16 See David Simmons, ed., *New Critical Essays on H. P. Lovecraft* (New York: Palgrave Macmillan, 2013) & Bobby Derie, *Sex and the Cthulhu Mythos* (New York: Hippocampus Press, 2014).

Goho's perceptive 'The Melancholia of H. P. Lovecraft's "The Music of Eric Zann"'; Michael D. Miller's cosmic '2001: A Lovecraftian Odyssey'; Bobby Derie's amusing 'That Fool Olson' and David Haden's illuminating '"Uncle Eddy": H. P. Lovecraft's Used Bookseller'.[17] The same goes for *New Directions in Supernatural Horror Literature: The Critical Influence of H. P. Lovecraft*, a 2018 anthology edited by Sean Moreland which provides new insights into Lovecraft's famous essay 'Supernatural Horror in Literature'.[18] Furthermore, I have enjoyed Jeb J. Card's 2019 book *Spooky Archaeology* and particularly chapter 10 labelled 'Cthulhu and Cosmic Mythology' because it focuses on archaeology and indeed the archaeologist in Lovecraft's work. I should also mention Martin Wangsgaard Jürgensen's 2020 *Skrækvisioner*. Written in Danish, my native tongue, it covers how Lovecraft contributed to the development of the modern horror story.[19] I should also draw attention to Michael Cisco who in 2021 published the informative *Weird Fiction: A Genre Study* examining themes including the supernatural, the bizarre and destiny in weird fiction as well as the socio-political implications of the genre.[20] Lastly, I would bring to attention the 2022 anthology *Lovecraft in the 21st Century* edited by Antonio Alcala Gonzalez and Carl H. Sederholm that looks at Lovecraft's influence in contemporary times from a wide range of perspectives.[21]

17 Dennis Quinn, 'Endless Bacchanal: Rome, Livy, and Lovecraft's Cthulhu Cult', in *Lovecraft Annual No. 5*, S. T. Joshi, ed. (New York: Hippocampus Press, 2011), 189–217; James Goho, 'The Melancholia of H. P. Lovecraft's "The Music of Eric Zann"', in *Lovecraft Annual No. 12*, S. T. Joshi, ed. (New York: Hippocampus Press, 2018), 3–12; Michael D. Miller, '2001: A Lovecraftian Odyssey', in *Lovecraft Annual No. 12*, S. T. Joshi, ed. (New York: Hippocampus Press, 2018), 75–89; Bobby Derie, 'That Fool Olson', in *Lovecraft Annual No. 12*, S. T. Joshi (New York: Hippocampus Press, 2018); and David Haden, '"Uncle Eddy": H. P. Lovecraft's Used Bookseller', in *Lovecraft Annual No. 16*, S. T. Joshi, ed. (New York: Hippocampus Press, 2022).

18 Sean Moreland, ed., *New Directions in Supernatural Horror Literature* (Palgrave Macmillan, 2018).

19 Jeb J. Card, *Spooky Archaeology* (Albuquerque: University of New Mexico Press, 2019) and Martin Wangsgaard Jürgensen *Skrækvisioner* (Syddanks Universitetsforlag, 2020).

20 Michael Cisco, *Weird Fiction: A Genre Study* (Palgrave Macmillan, 2021).

21 Antonio Alcala Gonzalez & Carl H. Sederholm, eds, *Lovecraft in the 21st Century: Dead, But Still Dreaming* (New York: Routledge, 2022).

In an introduction to a book such as *H. P. Lovecraft: Midnight Studies* it is fitting to say something about H. P. Lovecraft but given the rich biographical material readily available today I shall keep it somewhat brief and include a history of how I became fascinated by Lovecraft as a young man – a fascination that has stayed with me and indeed intensified as middle age hardened upon me.

Howard Phillips Lovecraft was born in 1890, in Providence, Rhode Island, on the American east coast. He was born into a wealthy family but ended his relatively short life in genteel poverty at the age of 46. Despite his brief life Lovecraft produced a staggering amount of literature in the form of poetry, weird fiction, essays and letters of which the latter amount to a number between 80,000 and 100,000.[22] Thus, in terms of letter output alone Lovecraft beats the prolific Bertrand Russell who produced approximately 40,000 letters in his lifetime, which in and of itself is almost an unfathomable feat.[23]

Lovecraft died in 1937 believing himself an underachiever if not a total failure, and literary critic Edmund Wilson, who in his 1945 article in *The New Yorker*: 'Tales of the Marvellous and the Ridiculous' labelled him a hack, somewhat confirmed this assessment.[24] However, like philosopher Friedrich Nietzsche and fellow writer and connoisseur of the extraordinary and fantastic Edgar Allan Poe who both enjoyed little fame and fortune during their lifetime, Lovecraft has achieved unquestionable posthumous fame. Today he is celebrated as an inspiration for everything from alcoholic beverages to blogs, books, clothing lines, films, graphic novels, music, plays, podcasts, role-playing, tabletop and video games. Lovecraft biographies are as mentioned plentiful and count among them L. Sprague de Camp's prominent *H. P. Lovecraft: A Biography*, Michel Houllebecq's influential *H. P. Lovecraft. Contre le Monde, Contre la Vie* and S. T. Joshi's two-volume tour de force: *I Am Providence: The Life and Times of H. P. Lovecraft.*

22 S. T. Joshi, 'A Look at Lovecraft's Letters', in *Primal Sources: Essays on H. P. Lovecraft* (New York: Hippocampus Press, 2003), 30.

23 Ray Monk, *Bertrand Russell: The Spirit of Solitude* (London: Jonathan Cape, 1996), xvii.

24 Edmund Wilson, 'Tales of the Marvelous and the Ridiculous', in *H. P. Lovecraft: Four Decades of Criticism*, S. T. Joshi, ed. (Athens: Ohio University Press, 1980), 46–49.

That Lovecraft is appreciated in our modern times is likewise evident from the fact that his work has been translated into multiple languages, including Danish, French, German and Japanese. One might also point out that Lovecraft enjoys the eponymous adjective: 'Lovecraftian' and that *Necronomicon* – an annual conference, taking place in Providence, Rhode Island – together with the S. T. Joshi Endowed Research Fellowship, connected to the John Hay Library at Brown University, where the world's largest collection of H. P. Lovecraft materials is kept, are both dedicated to him.

Personally, I first encountered Lovecraft's work in a local bookstore as a teenager. Being an ardent Stephen King reader in a time when there was no such thing as the Internet, I stopped by quite frequently to check if new works of horror had arrived. The bookstore, sporting a small horror section, already contained Grafton Books Omnibus series collecting Lovecraft's fiction, but despite being deeply fascinated by the lurid covers the content of these volumes eluded me because my English skills at the time were rather poor. However, a Danish translation of Lovecraft's 1941 short novel *The Case of Charles Dexter Ward* soon changed everything.[25] Published by Schønberg in 1991 in an uncut format and exhibiting a grinning human skull with a single illuminated eye on the cover it proved an utterly absorbing read, intensified by the fact that I for some unknown reason decided to cut the pages as I read on. The overall atmosphere of the novel transfixed me and the slow build-up of suspense, culminating perhaps in one of the greatest moments of Lovecraftian horror – the moment when Dr Willett discovers the horror in the pit underneath Wizard Curwen's squalid Pawtuxet bungalow – was astounding and left me with what I like to call a 'wondrous afterglow'. Now, a wondrous afterglow corresponds to a long-lasting mood involving a sense of gratitude and wondering expectancy; and today I am not only grateful to Lovecraft for his work but also that I in my youth stumbled upon the Schønberg translation.[26] Furthermore, whenever I engage with Lovecraft – be it reading one of his short stories or researching

25 See H. P. Lovecraft, *Tilfældet Charles Dexter Ward* (Århus: Schønberg, 1991).

26 Jan B. W. Pedersen, *Balanced Wonder: Experiential Sources of Imagination, Virtue, and Human Flourishing* (Lanham, MD: Lexington Books, 2019), 17, 149.

some aspects of his life – I always experience this slight tingling sensation as if a big secret is just around the corner waiting to be discovered. This, I believe, is equivalent to the 'wondering expectancy' mentioned above, and I dare say it has fuelled many late-night research activities – research activities crucial for the book at hand.

It is also appropriate in an introduction to a book to say something about its composition and the contents of each chapter. *H. P. Lovecraft: Midnight Studies* is philosophical and in this case hermeneutics and concept analysis are at the forefront because what you are about to read requires interpretation and addresses complex designations in need of unpacking including 'contemplation', 'Romanticism', 'teetotalism', 'virtue', 'the beautiful' and 'wonder', to name a few. Having said that, the book also draws on biography and indeed literary analysis without conforming to one specific type such as cultural, feminist or psychological analysis. The purpose of the book is as mentioned to introduce a Lovecraft full of Romantic sensibilities that so far have been overlooked in the literature and each chapter shows facets to support the idea of this other Lovecraft.

The book is divided into six chapters that can be read independently of each other and all the chapters except the final one which is entirely original consist in slightly revised versions of previously published material. Chapter 1, 'On Lovecraft's Lifelong Relationship with Wonder', was originally published in *Lovecraft Annual* No. 11 in 2017 and offers a preliminary exploration of Lovecraft's relationship with wonder. It highlights what wonder is, how Lovecraft was exposed to wonder at an early age, and argues that he developed a lifelong positive relationship with this state of mind. Importantly the chapter also connects Lovecraft with Romanticism – first and foremost via wonder, but also via his quest for poetic knowledge and indeed an analysis of Lovecraft's alter ego and dreamer extraordinaire: Randolph Carter.

Chapter 2, 'Howard Phillips Lovecraft: Romantic on the Nightside', was first published in *Lovecraft Annual* No. 12 in 2018 and can be viewed as a direct sequel to 'On Lovecraft's Lifelong Relationship with Wonder'. It gathers further evidence of Lovecraft's Romanticism and begins by adding to the earlier brief exploration of what Romanticism is only to move on to highlight elements of Romanticism in Lovecraft's poem 'Fact and Fancy'

(1917). My attention to the link between Lovecraft and Romanticism was invigorated when I noticed some striking similarities between Lovecraft's 'Fact and Fancy' and John Keats' poem 'Lamia'. Furthermore, Lovecraft's poem is curiously positive presenting a somewhat different Lovecraft than I had in mind at the time. The chapter concludes that, as much as Lovecraft can be labelled a Romantic based on his affinity with wonder, he can also be classified as such based on his aversion to the cold light of reason, which to him was an insufficient antidote to the dreary world in which he found himself.

Chapter 3, '"Now Will You Be Good?": Lovecraft, Teetotalism, and Philosophy', appeared in *Lovecraft Annual* No. 13 in 2019 and focuses on Lovecraft's aversion towards alcohol. It opens with a brief sketch of the historical background from which his dry outlook emerged and continues by providing evidence for Lovecraft's advocacy of abstinence and Prohibition from a variety of sources, including biographical material, philosophical essays, letters, poetry and fiction. The chapter shows how dramatically and intensely Lovecraft communicated his dry philosophy and how it softened as he advanced into middle age. The chapter ends by arguing that although there can be no doubt that Lovecraft was a teetotaller par excellence, his later softened position is more balanced and rooted partly in not only the realisation of his own idiosyncrasy and anachronism but also a change in his political outlook towards that of the Romantic.

Chapter 4, 'Lovecraft's Garden: Heart's Blood at the Root', was originally published in *Lovecraft Annual No. 16* in 2022. Romanticism is again in sharp focus, and it begins with a preliminary sketch of the use of gardens in Romantic thought and the highlighting of six themes: 'contemplation', 'joy', 'the dramatic', 'the strange', 'the foreign' and 'the beautiful', that all underpins Romanticism. This is followed by an elucidation of Lovecraft's fascination with gardens, his dealings in Romantic themes, and what role they play in his short 1917 poem 'A Garden'. The chapter concludes that given Lovecraft's love of gardens, and that his poem 'A Garden' is imbued with Romantic themes and involves 'wondrous contemplation' and 'poetic knowledge', the case for his Romanticism has been strengthened.

Chapter 5, 'Weird Fiction: A Catalyst for Wonder', began as a talk at the 2019 international conference *Wonder, Education, and Human*

Flourishing at Vrije Universiteit Amsterdam in the Netherlands. In 2020 it appeared in the open-access anthology *Wonder, Education, and Human Flourishing: Theoretical, Empirical, and Practical Perspectives* edited by Dr Anders Schinkel and published by VU University Press. Revised for the present book the chapter shows how weird fiction, understood as a sub-genre of speculative fiction, and particularly the work of H. P. Lovecraft is a catalyst for wonder. It takes the reader on a wonder-filled tour of Lovecraft's writings paying special attention to the presence of 'dark wonder' and the notion of Dark Romanticism. This is followed by some concluding remarks on the educational value of exposure to 'wonder' and 'dark wonder'.

Chapter 6, 'H. P. Lovecraft and The Dunsanian Conjuration', again focuses on Lovecraft's Romantic sensibilities and it pays attention to what the gentleman of Providence, in a somewhat paroxysmic epistle, phrased the 'Dunsanian Conjuration'. The chapter begins with a brief sketch of Lord Dunsany, the eponym of the phrase, and brings to the fore evidence of how Dunsany influenced Lovecraft. It continues with an exegesis showcasing what the 'Dunsanian Conjuration' is all about, followed by an apology arguing that the Dunsanian Conjuration has an honourable and practical use. The chapter concludes that Lovecraft as a Romantic via the Dunsanian Conjuration has granted us a useful tool that not only provides respite from a challenging existence but also a tool through which one might envision a better life and indeed gain inspiration to produce art.

I hope that each chapter will help you discover another Lovecraft, and that weirdness finds you while doing so. After all what is weird is wonderful and what is wonderful is not only full of wonders, it is also edifying and joyful. *Bonne lecture!*

Bibliography

Benson-Gyles, Dick, *The Boy in the Mask: The Hidden World of Lawrence of Arabia* (Dublin: The Lilliput Press, 2016).

Berlin, Isaiah, *The Roots of Romanticism*, Henry Hardy, ed. (Princeton, NJ: Princeton University Press, 2001).

Card, Jeb J., *Spooky Archaeology* (Albuquerque: University of New Mexico Press, 2019).

Cisco, Michael, *Weird Fiction: A Genre Study* (London: Palgrave Macmillan, 2021).

Derie, Bobby, *Sex and the Cthulhu Mythos* (New York: Hippocampus Press, 2014).

Gonzalez, Antonio Alcala & Sederholm, Carl H. eds, *Lovecraft in the 21st Century: Dead, But Still Dreaming* (New York: Routledge, 2022).

Harman, Graham, *Weird Realism: Lovecraft and Philosophy* (Winchester: Zero Books, 2012).

Joshi, S. T., ed., *H. P. Lovecraft: Four Decades of Criticism* (Athens: Ohio University Press, 1980).

Joshi, S. T., ed., *Lovecraft Annual No. 5* (New York: Hippocampus Press, 2011).

Joshi, S. T., ed., *Lovecraft Annual No. 12* (New York: Hippocampus Press, 2018).

Joshi, S. T., ed., *Lovecraft Annual No. 13* (New York: Hippocampus Press, 2019).

Joshi, S. T., ed., *Lovecraft Annual No. 16* (New York: Hippocampus Press, 2022).

Joshi, S. T., *Primal Sources: Essays on H. P. Lovecraft* (New York: Hippocampus Press, 2003).

Joshi, S. T. & Schultz, David E., *An H. P. Lovecraft Encyclopedia* (New York: Hippocampus Press, 2001).

Jürgensen, Martin Wangsgaard, *Skrækvisioner* (Odense: Syddansk Universitetsforlag, 2020).

Lovecraft, H. P., *Collected Essays: Volume 3: Science*, S. T. Joshi, ed. (New York: Hippocampus Press, 2005).

Lovecraft, H. P., *Collected Essays Volume 5: Philosophy, Autobiography & Miscellany*, S. T. Joshi, ed. (New York: Hippocampus Press, 2006).

Lovecraft, H. P., *Selected Letters II 1925–1929*, August Derleth & Donald Wandrei, eds (Sauk City, WI: Arkham House Publishers, 1968).

Lovecraft, H. P., *Selected Letters III 1929–1931*, August Derleth & Donald Wandrei, eds (Sauk City, WI: Arkham House Publishers, 1971).

Lovecraft, H. P., *The Ancient Track: The Complete Poetical Works of H. P. Lovecraft*, S. T. Joshi, ed. (New York: Hippocampus Press, 2013).

Lovecraft, H. P., *The New Annotated H. P. Lovecraft: Beyond Arkham*, Leslie S. Klinger, ed. (New York: Liveright Publishing Corporation, 2019).

Lovecraft, H. P., *Tilfældet Charles Dexter Ward* (Århus: Schønberg, 1991).

Machiavelli, Niccolò, *The Prince*, W. K. Marriot, trans. (Project Gutenberg, 1998).

Monk, Ray, *Bertrand Russell: The Spirit of Solitude* (London: Jonathan Cape, 1996).

Moreland, Sean, ed., *New Directions in Supernatural Horror Literature* (London: Palgrave Macmillan, 2018).

Pedersen, Jan B. W., *Balanced Wonder: Experiential Sources of Imagination, Virtue, and Human Flourishing* (Lanham, MD: Lexington Books, 2019).

Platon, Platon II: Samlede værker I ny oversættelse, Jørgen Mejer & Chr. Gorm Tortzen, eds (Copenhagen: Gyldendal, 2010).

Russell, Bertrand, *History of Western Philosophy* (London: Routledge, 2009).

Simmons, David, ed., *New Critical Essays on H. P. Lovecraft* (New York: Palgrave Macmillan, 2013).

Smith, Philip, 'Re-visioning Romantic-Era Gothicism: An Introduction to Key Works and Themes in the Study of H. P. Lovecraft, *Literature Compass* 8/11 (2021), 830–839.

Thacker, Eugene, *After Life* (Chicago: The University of Chicago Press, 2010).

Thacker, Eugene, *Horror of Philosophy*, vols 1–3 (Winchester: Zero Books, 2010/2015).

CHAPTER 1

On Lovecraft's Lifelong Relationship with Wonder

> When to this sense of fear and evil the inevitable fascination of wonder and curiosity is superadded, there is born a composite body of keen emotion and imaginative provocation whose vitality must of necessity endure as long as the human race itself.[1]

Howard Phillips Lovecraft's work of fiction can roughly be grouped into three distinct categories each evoking a singular extraordinary state of mind. Poe-inspired tales of the macabre such as 'The Tomb' (1917) and 'The Statement of Randolph Carter' (1920) produce terror because of the atmosphere they convey and because of the particular end the main characters meet. Lovecraft's later 'Yog-sothothery' or work in the Cthulhu Mythos tradition including his signature pieces of weird fiction 'The Call of Cthulhu' (1928) and 'The Shadow over Innsmouth' (1931) inspires 'horror' because the life-worlds of the protagonists in these stories are utterly destroyed. However, the gentleman of Providence is also known for a different sort of fiction. His Dunsanian tales counting among them short stories such as 'The White Ship' (1919), 'Celephaïs' (1920) and the three works: 'The Silver Key' (1929), 'Through the Gates of the Silver Key' (1934) and *The Dream-Quest of Unknown Kadath* (1948) centred on the exploits of Lovecraft's recurring character and alter ego Randolph Carter are epitomes to this feat.[2] These prehistoric or dreamland tales do

1 H. P. Lovecraft, 'Supernatural Horror in Literature', in *Collected Essays Volume 2: Literary Criticism*, S. T. Joshi, ed. (New York: Hippocampus Press, 2004), 83–84.

2 The label 'Dunsanian' links to Lord Dunsany also known as Edward Moreton Drax Plunkett who was the 18th Baron of Dunsany in Ireland and a fantasy writer. Among his many publications we find *The Book of Wonder* and *Tales of Wonder* of which the first Lovecraft thought essential to any basic weird library. See H. P. Lovecraft, 'Basic Books for a Weird Library', in *Collected Essays Volume 5: Philosophy, Autobiography & Miscellany*, S. T. Joshi, ed. (New York: Hippocampus Press, 2006), 264.

not so much inspire 'terror' or 'horror' but predominately seek to evoke the extraordinary state of mind called 'wonder'.[3]

The following offers a preliminary exploration of Lovecraft's relationship with wonder. It highlights what wonder is, how Lovecraft was exposed to wonder at an early age and argues that he developed a lifelong positive relationship with this particular state of mind.

What Is Wonder?

'Wonder' is a captivating interdisciplinary subject that has received increased academic attention in recent times. Over the last ten years new insightful literature has been added to *corpus admirans* including Sophia Vasalou's *Wonder A Grammer* (2015); Keagan Brewer's *Wonder and Skepticism in the Middle Ages* (2016); Robin Attfield's *Wonder, Value and God* (2017); Editors Christian Mieves and Irene Brown's, *Wonder in Contemporary Artistic Practice* (2017); Genevieve Lloyd's *Reclaiming Wonder After the Sublime* (2018); Catherine A. Racine's *Beyond Clinical Dehumanisation Towards the Other in Community Mental Health Care: Levinas, Wonder and Autoethnography* (2021) and Anders Schinkel's *Wonder and Education: On the Educational Importance of Contemplative Wonder* (2021). My own humble book *Balanced Wonder: Experiential Sources of Imagination, Virtue, and Human Flourishing* (2019) has likewise contributed to the literature on wonder.

The increased attention is understandable because as a subject of study 'wonder' is truly elusive and does not present itself as an external object that can be readily studied and explained by objective science. It is a human phenomenon, which can arise in a variety of situations. Witnessing a spectacle like the aurora borealis may induce wonder. The same can be said

3 It is difficult to conclude if Lovecraft's Dunsanian tales are set in the dream world or the real world. See S. T. Joshi, 'The Dream World and the Real World in Lovecraft', in *Primal Sources: Essays on H. P. Lovecraft* (New York: Hippocampus Press, 2003), 90–103.

of certain works of art including Guiseppe Arcimboldo's 1590 mannerist painting 'Four Seasons in One Head' and Les Edwards' 2010 black and white drawing of Celephaïs (see Figure 1.1). Even if one is not familiar with Lovecraft's eponymous story that inspired Edwards' drawing it provokes wonder because upon beholding the drawing questions concerning who the lonely figure is in the forefront, what he is doing there and why, spring to mind yet find no immediate answers. Further aesthetic appreciations would have us wonder about where the 'unknown' person actually is, why the cityscape is so curiously void of people and when the unknown person is there, because judging from the outlines of the city and the strange birds in the sky it is difficult to locate it in any particular time and place. Wonder has a particular history, which for most part is a tale of hyperbole and decline. In ancient Greece 'wonder' was connected to the divine. The poet Hesiod informs us that the sea god Thaumas (wonder) married Electra and had three daughters including Iris (rainbow) and the beautiful-haired harpies Aello and Ocypete.[4] Iris is important because she functions as messenger of the gods and as historian John Onians has pointed out she represents 'the supreme wonder, a miracle linking heaven and earth'.[5]

Wonder was also important to the Ancient Greek philosophers Plato and Aristotle who found wonder to be the feeling of the philosopher and the birthplace of philosophy.[6] Fast forward to the Enlightenment period the status of wonder slid into decline due to application of reason and empirical science and towards the end of the nineteenth century, around the time when Lovecraft was born, wonder had largely become associated with naivety and vulgarity in both Europe and America.

4 Hesiod, *Theogony, Works and Days, Testimonia*, Glenn W. Most, ed. & trans., Loeb Classical Library (Cambridge, MA: Harvard University Press, 1989),, 265.

5 See Hesiod, *Theogony*, 780, 784 & John Onians, 'I Wonder: A Short History of Amazement', in *Sight and Insight: Essays on Art and Culture in Honour of E. H. Combrich at 85*, John Onians, ed. (London: Phaidon Press, 1994), 32.

6 Plato, *Theaetetus*, 155d & Aristotle, *Metaphysics* I, II. 9.

Figure 1.1. Les Edwards, *Eldritch Tales: Celephaïs*, 2010. Courtesy of Les Edwards.

Throughout the twentieth century we can see sporadic upheavals of wonder and particularly in connection with the fantasy genre in literature. Here portrayed as an inner personal experience far removed from the outside world that science at the time had claimed as its focus wonder found a seemingly untouchable resting place.[7]

Earlier I said that wonder is a state of mind, but can we say something more specific about this singular state. I define wonder as sudden experience that intensifies the cognitive focus and awareness of ignorance about a given object.[8] It is typically an unsettling yet delightful experience that makes one aware that there might be more to the perceived object that meets

7 Dennis Quinn, *Iris Exiled: A Synoptic History of Wonder* (Lanham: University Press of America, 2002), 293–294.

8 Jan B. W. Pedersen, *Balanced Wonder: Experiential Sources of Imagination, Virtue, and Human Flourishing* (Lanham: Lexington Books, 2019), 1.

the eye. Because the imagination is intensified in wonderment, wonder may produce a range of effects including the widening of perspective, the development of an imaginative attitude and openness. Thus, the state of wonder is both singular and rewarding and it would seem a good idea to get in wonders way so to speak.

Early Exposure to Wonder

Lovecraft certainly got in wonders way and his intimate relationship with wonder started at an early age. His grandfather Whipple Van Buren Phillips had a preference for writers of gothic fiction such as Ann Radcliffe and Matthew Lewis and would entertain Lovecraft with wondrous oral tales of his own design.[9]

The spacious fifteen-room house on Angell Street in Providence was equally a source of wonder to the youthful Lovecraft because it contained an impressive library brought together by his well-read grandparents. The library contained a variety of classical literature, books on scientific matters and weird fiction of which many facilitated a sense of wonder in the young Lovecraft. At the age of 5, Lovecraft held *The Arabian Nights* in high esteem and, at age 6, he marvelled at the stories in Hawthorne's *Wonder Book* and *Tanglewood Tales.*[10]

We also know that the travel literature of Sir John Mandeville and Marco Polo had an impact on Lovecraft because through them he discovered the wonder of gaps, which in effect prevented him from committing suicide during his troubled adolescence. Lovecraft writes:

> As I contemplated an exit without further knowledge I became uncomfortably conscious of what I didn't know. Tantalising gaps existed everywhere [...] What of

9 L. Sprague de Camp, *Lovecraft: A Biography* (Garden City, NY: Doubleday, 1975), 17.

10 See H. P. Lovecraft, 'A Confession of Unfaith', in *Collected Essays Volume 5: Philosophy, Autobiography & Miscellany*, S. T. Joshi, ed. (New York: Hippocampus Press, 2006), 145.

the vast gulfs of space outside all familiar lands – desert reaches hinted by Sir John Mandeville & Marco Polo … Tartary, Thibet … What of unknown Africa? […] So in the end I decided to postpone my exit till the following summer.[11]

Figure 1.2. A Blemmyae depicted in historian Hartmann Schedel's *Nuremberg Chronicles* (1493).

11 See Lovecraft's 1934 letter to J. Vernon Shea in *H. P. Lovecraft Selected Letters IV 1932– 1934*, August Derleth & James Turner, eds (Sauk City, WI: Arkham House Publishers, 1976), 359. *The Arabian Nights* is important to Lovecraftians because it contains 'The History of Gherib and His Brother Agib' which harbours the earliest known reference to ghouls. The term ghoul was first mentioned in English literature in William Beckford's 1786 novel *Vathek* which Lovecraft had a copy of in his library and dedicates several paragraphs to it in his essay 'Supernatural Horror in Literature'. See S. T. Joshi, *Lovecraft's Library: A Catalogue*, 3rd edn (New York: Hippocampus Press, 2012), 29 & Lovecraft, 'Supernatural Horror in Literature', 93–94. Lovecraft's character, the painter Richard Upton Pickman introduced in the short story Pickman's Model (1927) recurs in *The Dream-Quest of Unknown Kadath* (1948) as a ghoul.

It is likely that the young Lovecraft through these travelogues also found inspiration to some of his later wondrous creations. In *The Travels of Sir John Mandeville,* we find lurid descriptions of ritual sacrifice and cannibalism, which are reoccurring themes in Lovecraft's stories. Mandeville also reports of wondrous creatures such as Sciapods (creatures with a single large foot), Blemmyaes (headless people with mouths in their chests and eyes on their shoulders) and flat- faced islands- folk without noses, eyes and lips (see Figure 1.2).

He even tells of people with feet like horses who run so swiftly they can overtake wild beasts and thus easily kill them.[12] Marco Polo's *The Travels* is no less marvellous because here we find descriptions of the great enchanters of Tibet who can 'summon up tempests, lightning and thunder, starting and stopping them at will'.[13] Fantastic creatures such as unicorns and hideous snakes of enormous size capable of swallowing a man in one gulp also feature.[14] No creature in Lovecraft's work fits the description of the strange monsters and weird folk from Mandeville and Polo precisely but Lovecraft's cannibalistic Ghasts who leap on hind legs and the supposedly cloven-hoofed men of Leng from *The Dream-quest of Unknown Kadath* (1948) could well have grown out of Lovecraft's infatuation with Mandeville. Likewise, there is a curious resemblance between the powers of the enchanters of Tibet that Polo speaks of, and the powers unleashed on top of Sentinel Hill in 'The Dunwich Horror' (1928) when the learned men from Arkham banish Wilbur Whateley's monstrous twin brother in an unexplainable cacophony of loud rumblings and lightning strikes.

12 See *The Travels of Sir John Mandeville*, C. W. R. D. Moseley, trans. (London: Penguin Books, 1983), 137.

13 Marco Polo, *The Travels*, Nigel Cliff, trans. (London: Penguin Books, 2015), 153.

14 Ibid., 159, 169.

Lifelong Wonder

Lovecraft entertained a positive attitude towards wonder throughout his life even though the world around him, thanks to the advancement of science became increasingly disenchanted. To give some weight to this claim let us look at a selection of passages from Lovecraft's diverse body of work that testifies to this effect starting with his early essay 'In Defence of Dagon' (1921):

> Pleasure to me is wonder – the unexplored, the unexpected, the thing that is hidden and the changeless thing that lurks behind superficial mutability. To trace the remote in the immediate; the eternal in the ephemeral; the past in the present; the infinite in the finite; these are to me the springs of delight and beauty.[15]

Lovecraft finds wonder pleasurable but also indicates that he is a Romantic treasuring exploration and the quest for poetic knowledge. This particular attitude is echoed in the short story 'The Nameless City' (1921) where the narrator's thirst for wonder trumps fear of the unknown and ushers him to enter the temple harbouring the opening to the remoter abysses.[16]

The lure of wonder is great but how can it possibly be more motivating than the fear of the unknown, which Lovecraft later in 1925 classifies as the oldest and strongest emotion of mankind?[17] To answer this question let us turn to the early modern French philosopher Rene Descartes. Descartes thought wonder to be the first of all the passions.[18] He held that when we find ourselves in a state of wonder as a result of encountering something new, we are not in a position to judge whether 'the new' is beneficial to us or not. We do not know whether the object of wonder will aid us or cause

15 H. P. Lovecraft, 'In Defence of Dagon', in *Collected Essays Volume 5: Philosophy, Autobiography & Miscellany*, S. T. Joshi, ed. (New York: Hippocampus Press, 2006), 53.

16 H. P. Lovecraft, 'The Nameless City', in *The New Annotated H. P. Lovecraft*, Leslie S. Klinger, ed. (New York: Liveright Publishing Corporation, 2014), 84.

17 Lovecraft, 'Supernatural Horror in Literature', 82.

18 Rene Descartes, 'The Passions of the Soul', in *The Philosophical Works of Descartes*, John Cottingham, trans. (Cambridge: Cambridge University Press, 1986), LIII.

us harm. In Lovecraft's story the Romantic narrator is oblivious as to what the temple holds and he does not know if it is to be loved, hated, desired or shunned, as each of these responses would depend on knowing whether the temple is useful or harmful, good or bad. In this way Cartesian wonder challenges fear as the oldest and strongest emotion of mankind.

Is it possible that Lovecraft was aware of this distinct Cartesian view of wonder at the time he was writing 'In Defence of Dagon' and 'The Nameless City'? In 1920 he wrote the short story 'From Beyond' (1934) which addresses distinctly Cartesian themes including our relationship with the external world and the 'mysterious' pineal gland. Now these themes are explored extensively in Descartes' 'The Passions of the Soul' but this particular work also contains Descartes' philosophy of emotion and his singular view of wonder. Thus, it is highly possible that Lovecraft knew about and even embraced Descartes' idea, that wonder is the first of the passions. Now if true, we have uncovered perhaps a new motive for why Lovecraft assigns wonder to be prima mobilia of the narrator in 'The Nameless City'. The narrator, as much as Lovecraft himself, is motivated by the first of all the passions, effectively qualifies as a searcher after wonder.

Lovecraft's affinity for wonder can also be detected in the short story Celephasïs (1922):

> There are not many persons who know what wonders are opened to them in the stories and visions of their youth; for when as children we listen and dream, we think but half-formed thoughts, and when as men we try to remember, we are dulled and prosaic with the poison of life. But some of us awake in the night with strange phantasms of enchanted hills and gardens, of fountains that sing in the sun, of golden cliffs overhanging murmuring seas, of plains that stretch down to sleeping cities of bronze and stone, and of shadowy companies of heroes that ride caparisoned white horses along the edges of thick forests; and then we know that we have looked back through the ivory gates into that world of wonder which was ours before we were wise and unhappy.[19]

19 H. P. Lovecraft, 'Celephaïs', in *The New Annotated H. P. Lovecraft: Beyond Arkham*, Leslie S. Klinger, ed. (New York: Liveright Publishing Corporation, 2019), 72.

The theme in this passage is perhaps not so much wonder but the loss of it and how certain people get a glimpse of a wonderful world beyond the everyday through their nightly dreams.

This particular trope can likewise be located in Lovecraft's fragment 'Azatoth' (1922). Here Lovecraft opens with: 'When age fell upon the world, and wonder went out of the minds of men' and then goes on to speak of an extraordinary man who escapes our modern world bereft of beauty when 'dream-haunted skies swelled down [...] and made him a part of their fabulous wonder'.[20]

Deliverance courtesy of powers beyond the waking world is explored to a greater extent in the short story 'The White Ship'. Here the protagonist Basil Elton, keeper of the North Point light and solitary wonderer par excellence encounters a 'rift in reality' in the form of the sea speaking to him about far distant lands. These marvellous goings-on intensify with the arrival of a white ship steered by a bearded old man and Elton's boarding of that ship via a bridge of moonbeams. From here they sail for the dreamworld and subsequently explore realms including the Land of Zar 'where dwell all the dreams and thoughts of beauty that come to men once and then are forgotten. Then Thalarion: 'The City of a Thousand Wonders, wherein reside all those mysteries that man has striven in vain to fathom.' Next up is Xura, 'the Land of Pleasures Unattained' and finally the land of fancy: Sona-Nyl where 'there is neither time nor space, neither suffering nor death'.[21] After spending many aeons in this wondrous utopia, Elton learns to covet the mysterious land of hope called Cathuria and after some time he persuades the captain of the White Ship to set sails once again and accompany him in the search for this unknown land. Following a blue celestial bird in the sky they leave the tranquil shores of Sona-Nyl only to find great loss because soon they face the edge of the world and a 'monstrous cataract wherein the oceans of the world drop down to abysmal nothingness'.[22] Darkness

20 H. P. Lovecraft, 'Azatoth', in *Eldritch Tales: A Miscellany of the Macabre*, Stephen Jones, ed. (London: Gollancz, 2011), 386–387.

21 H. P. Lovecraft, 'The White Ship', in *Eldritch Tales: A Miscellany of the Macabre*, Stephen Jones, ed. (London: Gollancz, 2011), 71–73.

22 Ibid., 75.

and two crashes follow. The first is accompanied by the 'shrieking of men and of things which were not men' and the second crash sees Elton opening his eyes upon the platform of the lighthouse. He learns that no time has passed since his departure to the dreamlands and that the lighthouse had failed to shine for the first time since his grandfather became its caretaker. At dawn he begins to look for wreckage but finds only the corpse of the celestial bird and that the ocean no longer speaks to him. We also learn that the White Ship never came again.

To continue the hunt for evidence of Lovecraft's occupation with wonder let us look at the sketch 'The History of the Necronomicon' (1927) and Olaus Wormius: the man responsible for the Latin translation of the *Necronomicon* – Lovecraft's infamous but fictional grimoire.[23] In real life Olaus Wormius was responsible for a Latin translation of *Regner Lodbrog's Epicedium*, a mythical eighth-century Danish manuscript originally written in runes that Lovecraft sought to improve.[24] Lovecraft might also have known about Wormius' occupation with wonders. To elaborate Olaus Wormius was a Danish sixteenth/seventeenth-century naturalist, physician and antiquarian famous for his Museum Wormianum – a wunderkammern or wonder-room also known as a cabinet of curiosity containing many marvellous things including the horn from a supposed unicorn as well as a multitude of exotic stuffed animals, minerals, plants and bizarre man- made objects (see Figure 1.3).

23 H. P. Lovecraft, 'The History of the Necronomicon', in *Eldritch Tales: A Miscellany of the Macabre*, Stephen Jones, ed. (London: Gollancz, 2011), 2.

24 S. T. Joshi, 'Lovecraft, Regner Logbrog, and Olaus Wormius', in *Primal Sources: Essays on H. P. Lovecraft* (New York: Hippocampus Press, 2003), 145, 152.

Figure 1.3. Title page of Olaus Wormius, Museum Wormianum seu Historia Renum Rariorum (Leiden, 1655).

On the first pages of 'The Silver Key' we meet the older Carter and indeed the mature Lovecraft. The opening pages read as a lament-full description of a world without wonder and bring to the forefront the hollowness Lovecraft felt about the dominating early twentieth-century nil admirari zeitgeist. No longer able to enter the gate of dreams Carter is forced to endure the familiarity of the commonplace and is looking to philosophy and science for consolation. Alas, this merely chains him down to things that are, and by learning about the workings of things mystery soon departs, leaving him disenchanted and hollow.[25] Upon revealing his dissatisfaction with this demystification of the world the scientists then seek to rehabilitate Carter's sense of wonder by urging him to 'find wonder in the atom's vortex and the mystery in the sky's

25 H. P. Lovecraft, 'The Silver Key', in *The Annotated H. P. Lovecraft*, Leslie S. Klinger, ed. (New York: Liveright Publishing Corporation, 2014), 158–159.

dimension'.[26] Carter, who sees no difference between the reality of the dreamworld and the reality of the 'real world' is unimpressed and is consequently stigmatised as immature and lacking in imagination.[27] In other words, the scientists' occupation with the-yet-to-be-described does not inspire wonder in the Romantic-orientated Carter and consequently he suffers ridicule much in the same way Lovecraft suffered ridicule for his writing. That Lovecraft had a low standing as an author to the point of ridicule is hinted at in his short story/satire 'The Unnameable' (1925) and very much confirmed by art critic Edmund Wilson in his 1945 article in the New Yorker entitled 'Tales of the Marvellous and the Ridiculous'.[28]

Mythos work such as 'The Shadow over Innsmouth' is likewise indicative of Lovecraft holding wonder in high esteem because despite the horror the protagonist undergoes the story ends somewhat happily. No longer caring about his transformation and Innsmouth-look the protagonist Robert Olmsted refrains from killing himself and instead expresses strong desires to go to 'marvel-shadowed Innsmouth' and dive down 'to Cyclopean and many columned Y'ha-nthlei' where he in the lair of the Deep Ones shall 'dwell amidst wonder and glory for ever'.[29] Like the narrator in 'The Nameless City', Olmsted has a Romantic mindset and at the end of the story casts aside his fear of change and transformation in favour of seeking wonder.

To give one last piece of evidence let us turn to Lovecraft's *Commonplace Book* which reveals that Lovecraft as late as 1934/1935 valued wonder and wonders. Entry number 208 reads:

> [Dream of] some vehicle – railway, coach, etc. – which is boarded in a stupor or fever, and which is a fragment of some past or ultra-dimensional world – taking

26 Ibid., 159.

27 Ibid., 159–160.

28 See H. P. Lovecraft, 'The Unnameable', in *The Annotated H. P. Lovecraft*, Leslie S. Klinger, ed. (New York: Liveright Publishing Corporation, 2014), 114 and Edmund Wilson, 'Tales of the Marvellous and the Ridiculous', in *H. P. Lovecraft: Four Decades of Criticism*, S. T. Joshi, ed. (Athens, OH: Ohio University Press, 1980), 46–49.

29 H. P. Lovecraft, 'The Shadow Over Innsmouth', in *The Annotated H. P. Lovecraft*, Leslie S. Klinger, ed. (New York: Liveright Publishing Corporation, 2014), 642.

> the passenger out of reality – into vague, age-crumbled regions or unbelievable gulfs of marvel.[30]

This entry shows not merely Lovecraft's imaginary powers but also his sense of wonder and ability to call up wonder in the mind of the reader. Despite its shortness the entry is delightful, and it is difficult not to wonder about what an ultra-dimensional world actually looks like; what it is to be out of reality and how to picture a vague, age-crumbled region or gulfs of marvel. The entry brings about an effect in league with the one prompted by 'Through the Gate of the Silver Key' where the reader is faced with multiple versions of Randolph Carter situated in different ages, realty outside time and the awful wonder of being Yog-Sothoth.[31]

Wonder-Loving Grandmothers and Lovecraft

Now I have spoken warmly about Lovecraft's lifelong positive relationship with wonder but biographical material and certain passages in his writing suggest that as much as he was fascinated with this particular state of mind, he was also aware of its 'dangers'.

Frank Belknap Long reports that in the early 1920s Lovecraft was an enthusiastic reader of the enlightenment poet Alexander Pope.[32] Pope delivers some of the harshest criticism of wonder in literature and it is quite possible that Lovecraft was familiar with it. In his *An Essay on Criticism* Pope states: 'For Fools admire, but men of sense approve' and in *The Sixth Epistle of the First Book of Horace* addressed to Mr Murray he writes: 'Not

30 H. P. Lovecraft, 'Commonplace Book', in *Collected Essays Volume 5: Philosophy, Autobiography & Miscellany*, S. T. Joshi, ed. (New York: Hippocampus Press, 2006), 232. Wonder and marvel are often used interchangeably.

31 H. P. Lovecraft with E. Hofmann Price, 'Through the Gate of the Silver Key', in *Eldritch Tales: A Miscellany of the Macabre*, Stephen Jones, ed. (London: Gollancz, 2011), 406–407.

32 Frank Belknap Long, *Howard Phillips Lovecraft: Dreamer on the Nightside* (Sauk City, WI: Arkham House Publishers, 1975), 92.

to admire is all the art I know, To make men happy, and to keep them so.'[33] The expression 'not to admire' is not coined by Pope himself but originates in the expression 'Nil Admirari' used in the *Epistles* written by the Roman poet Horace. Here Horace links the notion of Nil Admirari to human happiness by writing: 'Marvel at nothing – that is perhaps the one and only thing, Numicus, that can make a man happy and keep him so.'[34]

Pope's dismissive attitude towards wonder can be found in Lovecraft's character Albert N. Wilmarth, professor of literature at Miskatonic University and amateur folklorist featuring in the novelette 'The Whisperer in Darkness' (1930). In the beginning Lovecraft has Wilmarth use the singular phrase 'wonder-loving grandmothers', which in and of itself ridicules wonder (and indeed grandmothers) and portrays it as a state of mind that only fools would adhere to. This reflects Pope's dismissive and hostile attitude towards wonder and the fact that Lovecraft uses it in a story to give an aura of scepticism to a scholarly protagonist suggests that he was well aware that wonder can lead a person astray and that wonder as a motivator for inquiry found little support amongst the academically inclined of his time.

Summary: The Unsung Worshipper of Iris

From the above it is clear that Lovecraft was exposed to the extraordinary state of mind we call wonder quite early in his life. The old house on Angell Street, the weird oral tales of his grandfather and the numerous wondrous books in the family library including *The Arabian Nights*, Hawthorne's *Wonder Book* and *Tanglewood Tales, The Travels of Sir Mandeville* and Marco Polo's *The Travels* all have prominent parts to play

33 See Alexander Pope, 'An Essay on Criticism' & 'The Sixth Epistle of The First Book of Horace', in *The Poetic Works of Alexander Pope*, A. W. Ward, ed. (London: Macmillan, 1885), 59; I. 393 & 300; III. 1–2. Wonder and admiration are sometimes used interchangeably.

34 Horace, *Epistle* VI in *Satires, Epistles, Ars Poetica*, H. R. Fairclough, trans., Loeb Classical Library (Cambridge, MA: Harvard University Press, 1955), 287.

in the development of what was to be a lifelong fascination with wonder for Lovecraft.

Searchers after wonder in Lovecraft will do well to look to his Dunsanian stories and here I have but briefly examined a handful of these including 'Azatoth', 'The White Ship', 'Celephaïs' and 'The Silver Key'. However, Lovecraft's Mythos stories are not without the touch of wonder. 'The Shadow Over Innsmouth' clearly indicates Lovecraft's fascination with wonder towards the end and 'The Nameless City' is captivating because here wonder trumps fear of the unknown as the narrator's primary driving force. Sketches such as 'The History of the Necronomicon' and entries in Lovecraft's *Commonplace Book* such as entry 208 are likewise suggestive of Lovecraft's wonder-filed mind but it is perhaps in his essay 'In Defence of Dagon' we find his most affectionate dedication to wonder. Here readers of Lovecraft believing him purely to be a man of terror and horror must yield to a much more complex picture and acknowledge that the gentleman of Providence was as much a worshipper of Iris as a lover of the sense of fear and evil. His Romantic heart would leap up if he beheld a rainbow in the sky as much as it would sink for every rejection or insult, he suffered as an author of low standing.

Bibliography

Aristotle, *Metaphysics*, Hugh Tredennick, trans., Loeb Classical Library (Cambridge, MA: Harvard University Press, 1933).

Attfield, Robin, *Wonder, Value and God* (London: Routledge, 2017).

Brewer, Keagan, *Wonder and Skepticism in the Middle Ages* (London: Routledge, 2016).

De Camp, L. Sprague, *Lovecraft: A Biography* (New York: Doubleday, 1975).

Descartes, Rene, *The Philosophical Works of Descartes*, vol. 1, John Cottingham, trans. (Cambridge: Cambridge University Press, 1985).

Hesiod, *Theogony, Works and Days, Testimonia*, Glenn W. Most, ed. & trans., Loeb Classical Library (Cambridge, MA: Harvard University Press, 1989).

Horace, *Satires, Epistles, Ars Poetica*, H. R. Fairclough, trans., Loeb Classical Library (Cambridge, MA: Harvard University Press, 1955).

Joshi, S. T., *Lovecraft's Library: A Catalogue*, 3rd edn (New York: Hippocampus Press, 2012).

Joshi S. T., *Primal Sources: Essays on H. P. Lovecraft* (New York: Hippocampus Press, 2003).

Lloyd, Genevieve, *Reclaiming Wonder after the Sublime* (Edinburgh: Edinburgh University Press, 2018).

Lovecraft, H. P., *Collected Essays Volume 2: Literary Criticism*, S. T. Joshi, ed. (New York: Hippocampus Press, 2004).

Lovecraft, H. P., *Collected Essays Volume 5: Philosophy, Autobiography & Miscellany*, S. T. Joshi ed. (New York: Hippocampus Press, 2006).

Lovecraft, H. P., *Selected Letters IV 1932–1934*, August Derleth & James Turner, eds (Sauk City, WI: Arkham House Publishers, 1976).

Lovecraft, H. P., *The New Annotated H. P. Lovecraft*, Leslie S. Klinger, ed. (New York: Liveright Publishing Corporation, 2014).

Lovecraft, H. P., *The New Annotated H. P. Lovecraft: Beyond Arkham*, Leslie S. Klinger, ed. (New York: Liveright Publishing Corporation, 2019).

Mieves, Christian & Brown, Irene, eds, *Wonder in Contemporary Artistic Practice* (London: Routledge, 2017).

Onians, John, ed., *Sight and Insight: Essays on Art and Culture in Honour of E. H. Combrich at 85* (London: Phaidon Press, 1994).

Pedersen, Jan B. W., *Balanced Wonder: Experiential Sources of Imagination, Virtue, and Human Flourishing* (Lanham: Lexington Books, 2019).

Plato, *Theaetetus*, H. N. Fowler, trans., Loeb Classical Library (Cambridge, MA: Harvard University Press, 1989).

Polo, Marco, *The Travels*, Nigel Cliff, trans. (London: Penguin Books, 2015).

Pope, Alexander, *The Poetic Works of Alexander Pope*, A. W. Ward, ed. (London: Macmillan, 1885).

Quinn, Dennis, *Iris Exiled: A Synoptic History of Wonder* (Lanham: University Press of America, 2002).

Racine, Catherine A., *Beyond Clinical Dehumanisation towards the Other in Community Mental Health Care: Levinas, Wonder and Autoethnography* (London: Routledge, 2021).

Schinkel, Anders, *Wonder and Education: On the Educational Importance of Contemplative Wonder* (London: Bloomsbury Academic, 2021).

The Travels of Sir John Mandeville, C. W. R. D. Moseley, trans. (London: Penguin Books, 1983).

Vasalou, Sophia, *Wonder a Grammar* (New York: Suny Press, 2015).

CHAPTER 2

Howard Phillips Lovecraft: Romantic on the Nightside

In the previous chapter we saw that Howard Phillips Lovecraft can be viewed as a Romantic based on his lifelong relationship with wonder. This chapter gathers further evidence of Lovecraft's Romanticism and begins with a brief exploration of what Romanticism is and then moves on to highlight elements of Romanticism in Lovecraft's poem 'Fact and Fancy' (1917). The chapter concludes that as much as Lovecraft can be labelled a Romantic based on his affinity with wonder, he can also be classified as such based on his aversion to the cold light of reason, which to him was an insufficient antidote to the dreary world he found himself thrown into.

What Is Romanticism?

Etymologically speaking Romanticism comes from the word 'Roman' which in English translates into 'novel' – a work of fiction or a 'romance'.[1] Romanticism can be understood as a countermovement to Enlightenment thought, which gained momentum approximately between 1760 and 1850 in Europe. By and large it was an artistic movement that voiced itself through music, poetry, dance, literature and painting.[2]

1 See Carl Schmitt, *Political Romanticism*, Guy Oakes, trans. (Cambridge, MA: MIT Press, 2011), 30. In Danish 'a novel' is called 'en roman' and in the German language 'a novel' translates into 'der Roman'.

2 Christopher John Murray, ed., *Encyclopedia of the Romantic Era: 1760–1850*, vol. 1 (New York: Routledge, 2003), ix.

The Romantics criticised the core of the Enlightenment which according to philosopher Isaiah Berlin covers the following three propositions: (1) all genuine questions can be answered, (2) the answers are knowable and (3) the answers must be compatible with one another.[3] To elaborate one might say that the Enlightenment thinker believed that the way natural philosopher Isaac Newton (1642–1726–1727) had mastered the domain of physics could also be used in the realms of ethics, politics and aesthetics. Questions about how to live, how to build a perfect society and how to judge something as beautiful or ugly could be answered simply by applying reason. Now the Romantics thought this a terrible mistake because the Enlightenment thinkers simply failed to do justice to the role of emotion, feeling and intuition in domains of meaning and value.

To showcase this particular aspect of Romantic thought let us turn to Romantic poet John Keats (1795–1821) who writes:

> Do not all charms fly
>
> At the mere touch of cold philosophy?
>
> There was an awful rainbow once in the heaven:
>
> We know her woof, her texture: she is given
>
> In the dull catalogue of common things.
>
> Philosophy will clip an Angel's wings,
>
> Conquer all mysteries by rule and line,
>
> Empty the haunted air, and gnomed mine–
>
> Unweave a rainbow, as it erewhile made
>
> The tender-personed Lamia melt into a shade[4]

In Keats's 'Lamia' we find evidence of his critical attitude towards natural philosophy, which one might understand as a precursor to modern

3 Berlin, *The Roots of Romanticism*, 21–22.

4 John Keats, 'Lamia', in *The Complete Poems of John Keats*, John Barnard, ed. (Penguin Books, 1988), II, 229–238.

science.[5] The scientifically inclined will recall that Newton successfully replicated the rainbow in his studies of prisms thus stripping away its mystery and to Keats this was nothing short of the destruction of the poetry of the rainbow.[6] Newton's prism exorcised the wondrous Iris, messenger of the gods in Greek mythology from the rainbow. It hollowed it out, stripped it of a valuable quality and reduced it to a vacuum wrapped in colours.

Another Romantic that called into question the disenchanting attitude of the Enlightenment is the mad, bad and dangerous to know poet Lord Byron (1788–1824).[7] In the satirical poem 'Don Juan' he curiously states that he 'never could see the very Great Happiness of the Nil Admirari'.[8] Now 'Nil Admirari' is a cautionary Latin phrase originating in the writings of Roman poet Horace and much used by Enlightenment poet Alexander Pope. It basically urges us not to marvel, wonder or admire because being in such a state of mind is distracting, useless and dangerous to the person of knowledge. The poem continues with not merely a salutation to Horace and Pope but also a strong counterargument that disputes the reasonableness of the 'Nil Admirari' mindset. It reads:

> Not to admire is all the art I know
>
> (Plain truth, dear Murray, needs few flowers of speech)
>
> To make men happy, or to keep them so;
>
> (So take it in the very words of Creech).
>
> Thus Horace wrote we all know long ago;
>
> And this Pope quotes the precept to re-teach

5 'Lamia' is the name of a being from Greek Mythology that started out, as a woman but became a child-eating monster after the Olympian Hera destroyed her children.

6 Dennis Quinn, *Iris Exiled—A Synoptic History of Wonder* (Lanham: University Press of America, 2002), 270.

7 The phrase 'mad, bad and dangerous to know' was used by Lady Caroline Lamb to describe Lord Byron whom she had an affair with in 1812. See Fiona MacCarthy, *Byron: Life and Legend* (New York: Farrar, Straus and Giroux, 2002), 164.

8 Lord Byron, 'Don Juan', in *The Works of Lord Byron* (London: John Murray, 1833), canto V, 100.

From his translation; but had *none admired*,

Would Pope have sung, or Horace been inspired?[9]

What Byron's is telling us is that if we cannot wonder we will never find inspiration and if Pope never wondered at the poetry of Horace his Horace-inspired poetry would never have seen the light of day. Thus in Byron's view poetry cannot rely on reason alone but must begin in wonder.

Byron's dislike of the 'Nil Admirari' stance points out an important feature of Romanticism – a point that the Romantic poet William Wordsworth (1770–1850) shared. Now Wordsworth was not against science as such, but he warned his readers against the cold detachment associated with it and its obsceneness – its perversion. In 'A Poet's Epitaph' he writes:

Physician art thou? – one, all eyes,

Philosopher! – a fingering slave.

One that would peep and botanize

Upon his mother's grave?[10]

To Wordsworth the natural philosopher is an obscene and perverse creature because not only is he a slave to his cold detached outlook he is also willing to investigate areas that should not be touched. He is the equivalent of a peeping Tom – a curious creature devoid of wonder showing no restraints whatsoever.[11] Such a creature is not only immoral but also

9 Ibid., canto V, 101.

10 William Wordsworth, 'A Poet's Epitaph', in *William Wordsworth: The Major Works*, Stephen Gill, ed. (Oxford: Oxford University Press), 151.

11 Curiosity and wonder can be used interchangeably but it is also possible to view them as distinct. In contemporary times we tend to view curiosity as something positive and wonder as something associated with naivety but in the medieval period things were quite the opposite. Curiosity was back then seen as morally ambiguous, and something closely related to an insatiable desire prompting people to mingle in affairs that were not their concern. Wonder on the other hand were viewed with reverence. For more information see Lorraine Daston & Katharine Park, *Wonders and the Order of Nature* (New York: Zone Books, 1998), 31 and my book *Balanced Wonder: Experiential Sources of Imagination, Virtue, and Human Flourishing* (Lanham: Lexington Books, 2019), 48–49.

dangerous which is a theme Romantic writer Mary Shelley elegantly used in her Gothic 1818 novel *Frankenstein or, The Modern Prometheus.*[12]

As mentioned, Romanticism can be seen as a countermovement to Enlightenment thought and the detached enlightenment scientist entertaining a disregard or belittling of emotions and enthusiasm was to the Romantic an absolute abomination. The Romantic revolt resulted in a 'Cartesian split' between science and poetry meaning that science in the name of reason would continue the exploration of *res extensa*, the material universe while poetry would exercise dominion over *res cogitans* meaning everything from the heart to beauty, imagination, the good, spirit and of course wonder – that special feeling associated with the philosophers of ancient times.[13]

Romanticism in Lovecraft's 'Fact and Fancy'

In the first chapter we saw that evidence of Lovecraft's Romanticism can be found in early essays such as *In Defence of Dagon* (1921) and works of fiction including 'The Nameless City' (1921). However Romantic thought is also to be found in Lovecraft's poetry and in particular the poem 'Fact and Fancy', which in its entirety reads as follows:

> How dull the wretch, whose philosophic mind
> Disdains the pleasures of fantastic kind;
> Whose prosy thoughts the joys of life exclude,
> And wreck the solace of the poet's mood!
> Young Zeno, practic'd in the Stoic's art,
> Rejects the language of the glowing heart;
> Dissolves sweet Nature to a mess of laws;
> Condemns th' effect whilst looking for the cause;

12 Mary Shelley, *Frankenstein or, The Modern Prometheus* (London: Collectors Library, 2004).

13 Plato, *Theaetetus*, 155d.

Freezes poor Ovid in an ic'd review,
And sneers because his fables are untrue!
In search of Truth the hopeful zealot goes,
But all the sadder turns, the more he knows!
Stay! vandal sophist, whose deep lore would blast
The graceful legends of the story'd past;
Whose tongue in censure flays th' embellish'd page,
And scolds the comforts of a dreary age:
Would'st strip the foliage from the vital bough
Till all men grow as wisely dull as thou?
Happy the man whose fresh, untainted eye
Discerns a Pantheon in the spangled sky;
Finds Sylphs and Dryads in the waving trees,
And spies soft Notus in the southern breeze;
For whom the stream a cheering carol sings,
While reedy music by the fountain rings;
To whom the waves a Nereid tale confide
Till friendly presence fills the rising tide.
Happy is he, who void of learning's woes,
Th' ethereal life of body'd Nature knows:
I scorn the sage that tells me it but seems,
And flout his gravity in sunlit dreams![14]

The opening bears a resemblance in both mood and contents to the excerpt from Keats' 'Lamia' we saw earlier. Both poems criticise the philosophically inclined but where Keats directs his aversion towards the natural philosopher or scientist who in cold blood will clip an angel's wings, empty the haunted air and unweave the rainbow by rule and line (scientific method) Lovecraft airs his aversion towards philosophy because it wrecks the solace of the poet's mood with its prosy thoughts and negative attitude towards pleasures of the fantastic.

Lovecraft then takes a swing at the 'ever sadder' Hellenistic stoic philosopher Zeno whom he claims cares not for the 'language of the glowing heart' (poetry) and by focussing on causality reduces 'Nature'

14 H. P. Lovecraft, 'Fact and Fancy', in *The Ancient Track: The Complete Poetical Works of H. P. Lovecraft*, S. T. Joshi, ed. (New York: Hippocampus Press, 2013), 121.

to a mess of laws.[15] 'Nature' clearly has a particular meaning and value for Lovecraft that he feels Stoicism undermines and this could well be rooted in a deep Romantic wish for the world to be enchanted.

In Ancient and Hellenistic times, the great god Pan was not only a being in the woods that occasionally scared humans and animals alike or made them 'panic' but could also represent the 'whole of nature' or 'everything', which the word 'pan' may also refer to in Greek. In this sense nature is not an empty concept but very much a word that evokes the mysterious and the divine. Now two things are important here: First we know that Pan was much valued by the early Lovecraft because his poem 'To Pan' (1919) published under the pseudonym Michael Ormonde O'Reilly celebrates the deity in question and reveals Lovecraft's longing for living in an enchanted world filled with Nymphs and Satyrs. Likewise, the poem 'To the Old Pagan Religion' (1919) published under the pseudonym Ames Dorrance Rowley reveals his affinity for Greek mythology because it opens with the line: 'Olympian Gods! How can I let ye go and pin my faith on this new Christian creed?'[16]

'Fact and Fancy' likewise reveals Lovecraft's longing for a world filled with gods away from cold philosophy because in line 9–10 he states that Stoicism 'Freezes poor Ovid in an ic'd review, And sneers because his fables are untrue'. Now Publius Ovidius Naso (43 BC–17/18 AD) or Ovid as the English-speaking world came to address him was a Roman poet who ended his life in exile shrouded in mystery. He is particularly known for his fifteen-book-long epic (or type of epic) magnum opus the *Metamorphoseon Libri* (books of transformations) which with playful wit covers a vast amount of myths and delivers intricate portrayals of mythic figures – from Minerva and Arachne to Orpheus in the Underworld. We know that Ovid had some influence

15 None of Zeno's works have survived in their entirety. We do know some of the titles he used and have several fragmentary quotations available in the works of later writers including Roman philosopher Cicero (106 BC–43 AD) and biographer Diogenes Laërtius (third century AD).

16 H. P. Lovecraft, 'To the Old Pagan Religion', in *The Ancient Track: The Complete Poetical Works of H. P. Lovecraft*, S. T. Joshi, ed. (New York: Hippocampus Press, 2013), 31.

on nineteenth-century Romanticism because the poet Charles Pierre Baudelaire wrote an essay on his life and exile thus giving rise to the idea that Ovid was a misunderstood genius, which was an important theme in Romantic thought.[17]

That the polytheistic world of the ancients was important to the gentle poet of Providence also emerges in line 19–20 of 'Fact and Fancy' where Lovecraft writes 'Happy the man whose fresh, untainted eye discerns a Pantheon in the spangled sky'.[18]

The second important thing is that although Stoics like Zeno operated with a notion of the divine, they never evoked mysterious entities like Pan or Iris but thought of it in the abstract and as something 'absent' from our daily lives. For Zeno the cosmos as a whole was a living thing and God a corporeal and immanent living fire or heat with a development plan moving the world towards a fiery cataclysm followed by rebirth. Though still pantheistic this is far from the enchanted world Lovecraft dreamed about because as he writes towards the end of 'Fact and Fancy': 'Happy is he, who void of learning's woes, Th' ethereal life of body'd Nature knows.'[19]

17 See Matt Cartmill, *A View to a Death in the Morning: Hunting and Nature Through History* (Harvard University Press, 1996), 118–119. Baudelaire (1821–1867) influenced Lovecraft which is evident when we read the short story 'Hypnos' (1923) which opens with a verse from Baudelaire. Additional greetings to Baudelaire can be located in the short story 'The Hound' (1924). The notion of the misunderstood genius is to some extend explored by Lovecraft in his dreamland stories involving the mystic, scholar, author and dreamer extraordinaire Randolph Carter.

18 Lovecraft, 'Fact and Fancy', 121, 19–20.

19 Ibid., 121, 27–28.

Figure 2.1. Les Edwards, *The Necronomicon: The Reef*, 2007. Courtesy of Les Edwards.

That learning is the bringer of woes is a reoccurring theme in many a Lovecraft story including 'From Beyond' (1934) and 'The Call of Cthulhu' (1928). Here a hitherto unseen 'horror-world' is brought before the protagonist with destructive consequences either by marvellous machinery or the art of 'piecing together'.

In 'Fact and Fancy' the horror of learning is altogether different in colour and suggestion because it does not so much add a dimension to the ordinary understanding of things but rather takes one away. No inky jellyish monstrosities suddenly fill the blue sky nor is one all of a sudden confronted by eldritch contradictions of all matter, force and cosmic order. Instead in Lovecraft's view one is bereaved as the Stoic takes the ethereal poetical element out of nature thus reducing it to nothing but a bundle of soulless laws bereft of wonder and the fantastic. Lovecraft's Zeno is what the observing physician and slavish philosopher are to Wordsworth and what the Nil Admirari supporter is to Byron. He is the destroyer of worlds enchanted, the enemy of Romanticism and what the smell of fish was to Lovecraft: Utterly insufferable!

Speaking of fish 'Fact and Fancy' ends in Romantic revolt, not unlike the ending of the mythos story 'The Shadow Over Innsmouth' (1931) where the protagonist, Robert Olmstead, filled with renewed vigour, refrains from killing himself upon discovering that he will turn into a blasphemous fish-frog (see Figure 2.1).[20] 'I scorn the sage that tells me it but seems and flout his gravity in sunlit dreams' is a surprisingly uplifting rally to fancy and a wholesomely defiant stance from Lovecraft. It bears witness to the fact that he not only detested the philosophy of the Stoic sage like Byron detested the philosophy of Pope but that his use of fancy, imagination or the 'poet's eye' is a means to dispel the gravity of the wise and unhappy. As much as poetry can convey a particular message, it is also transformative and the ending of 'Fact and Fancy' bears witness to Lovecraft poetic acumen. In two lines he re-installs the dimension the learned Stoic took away and we are left with an impression of Lovecraft as a jovial and positive fellow. A resourceful person we can look to for comfort when darkness or emptiness is closing in.

Summary: Thus Spoke Lovecraft the 'Poe'-et

Based on the above analysis I think that 'Fact and Fancy' testifies to Lovecraft's Romanticism. The resemblance between Keats's 'Lamia' and Lovecraft's 'Fact and Fancy' is striking and it is likely that Keats' poem was a source of inspiration to the gentleman of Providence. Lovecraft definitively knew about 'Lamia' because it is mentioned in his singular essay 'Supernatural Horror in Literature' (1927). That he was aware of other works by Keats is also evident because the opening epigram of the short story 'The Outsider' (1926) is an excerpt from Keats' narrative poem 'The Eve of St. Agnes'.

Now it is a well-established fact that Lovecraft was a great admirer of Edgar Allan Poe. In 1916 – a year before Lovecraft published 'Fact and Fancy' – Lovecraft wrote in a letter to Reinhardt Kleiner that Poe was his

20 Lovecraft, 'The Shadow Over Innsmouth', 641.

'God of Fiction' and early tales of the macabre such as 'The Tomb' (1917) and 'The Statement of Randolph Carter' (1919) conveys a positively Poesque atmosphere.[21] Poe's poem 'Sonnet – To Science' bears a curious resemblance to Keat's 'Lamia' because where Keats' laments that the cold touch of philosophy has put the awful rainbow in the dull catalogue of common things Poe laments that science 'whose wings are dull realities' preys on the poet's heart.[22] This equals Lovecraft's statement that philosophy wrecks the solace of the poet's mood by reducing nature to laws and thus it may be speculated that 'Fact and Fancy only is inspired indirectly by Keats's 'Lamia and is inspired directly by Poe's 'Sonnet – To Science'. Regardless of if this is true or not 'Fact and Fancy' is a Romantic poem as much as 'Lamia' and 'Sonnet – To Science' are and it leaves us with the impression that Howard Phillips Lovecraft, at heart, was a Romantic deeply at odds with the cold light of reason that was an uninspiring and inadequate antidote to the dreary world in which he was situated. He was a Romantic that, in light of his immense contribution to weird fiction, is perhaps best addressed as a Romantic on the 'Nightside'.[23]

Bibliography

Berlin, Isaiah, *The Roots of Romanticism*, Henry Hardy, ed. (Princeton, NJ: Princeton University Press, 2001).

Byron, Lord George Gordon, *The Works of Lord Byron* (London: John Murray, 1833).

Cartmill, Matt, *A View to a Death in the Morning: Hunting and Nature through History* (Cambridge, MA: Harvard University Press, 1996).

21 See Lovecraft's 1916 letter to Reinhardt Kleiner in H. P. Lovecraft, *Selected Letters I 1911–1924*, August Derleth & Donald Wandrei, eds (Sauk City, WI: Arkham House Publishers, 1965), 20.

22 See Edgar Allan Poe, *The Complete Poetry of Edgar Allan Poe* (New York: Signet, 2008), 45.

23 I borrowed the term 'Nightside' from Frank Belknap Long's 1975 biography: *Howard Phillips Lovecraft: Dreamer on the Nightside* (Sauk City, WI: Arkham House Publishers, 1975).

Daston, Lorraine & Park, Katharine, *Wonders and the Order of Nature* (New York: Zone Books, 1998).

Keats, John, *The Complete Poems of John Keats*, John Barnard, ed. (London: Penguin Books, 1988).

Long, Frank Belknap, *Howard Phillips Lovecraft: Dreamer on the Nightside* (Sauk City, WI: Arkham House, 1975).

Lovecraft, H. P., *Selected Letters I 1911–1924*, August Derleth & Donald Wandrei, eds (Sauk City, WI: Arkham House Publishers, 1965).

Lovecraft, H. P., *The Ancient Track: The Complete Poetical Works of H. P. Lovecraft*, S. T. Joshi, ed. (New York: Hippocampus Press, 2013).

Lovecraft, H. P., *The Annotated H. P. Lovecraft*, Leslie S. Klinger, ed. (New York: Liveright Publishing Corporation, 2014).

MacCarthy, Fiona, *Byron: Life and Legend* (New York: Farrar, Straus and Giroux, 2002).

Murray, Christopher John, ed., *Encyclopedia of the Romantic Era: 1760–1850*, vol. 1 (New York: Routledge, 2003).

Plato, *Theaetetus*, H. N. Fowler, trans., Loeb Classical Library (Cambridge, MA: Harvard University Press, 1989).

Poe, Edgar Allan, *The Complete Poetry of Edgar Allan Poe* (New York: Signet, 2008).

Quinn, Dennis, *Iris Exiled: A Synoptic History of Wonder* (Lanham: University Press of America, 2002).

Schmitt, Carl, *Political Romanticism*, Guy Oakes, trans. (Cambridge, MA: MIT Press, 2011).

Shelley, Mary, *Frankenstein or, The Modern Prometheus* (London: Collectors Library, 2004).

Wordsworth, William, *William Wordsworth: The Major Works*, Stephen Gill, ed. (Oxford: Oxford University Press, 2008).

CHAPTER 3

'Now Will You Be Good?': Lovecraft, Teetotalism and Philosophy

> It is an aesthetic matter with me. I think drink is ugly, & therefore I have nothing to do with it.[1]

Lovecraft's teetotalism is well known among Lovecraftians but the lengths to which he went to incorporate his views and how he sought to influence the people around him via his various writing remains relatively unexplored.[2] This chapter focuses on Lovecraft's teetotalism and opens with a brief sketch of the historical backdrop from which his dry outlook emerged. It continues by providing evidence for Lovecraft's advocacy of abstinence and Prohibition from a variety of sources, including biographical material, philosophical essays, letters, poetry and fiction, with a view to show how he communicated his dry philosophy and how it softened over time. The chapter ends by arguing that although there can be no doubt that Lovecraft was a teetotaller par excellence, his later moderated position is not only rooted in the realisation of his own idiosyncrasy and anachronism but also inspired by Romantic political thought.

1 See Lovecraft's letter dated 13 February 1928 to Zealia Brown Reed Bishop in *The Spirit of Revision: Lovecraft's Letters to Zealia Brown Reed Bishop*, Sean Branney & Andrew Leman, eds (HPLHS, 2015), 104–105.

2 Ironically Lovecraft has in recent years inspired certain alcoholic beverage companies to produce a wide range of eldritch sounding drinks. The Narragansett Beer Company's *Lovecraft series* is currently sporting exquisite beers including *Innsmoouth Old Ale, Reanimator Helles Lager, The Unnameable Black Lager,* and *White Ship*. They also offer *Lovecraft Hopped Whiskey*.

Against a Drunken Background: England

Lovecraft was an Anglophile, and his teetotalism is connected to his beloved English heritage.[3] In seventeenth-century England drunkenness was generally perceived as a benign and laughable condition. However, by the eighteenth century, and particularly with the advent of the Gin-Craze in the 1720s, the face of drunkenness changed. New laws intended to boost the economy permitted everyone to produce gin from English cereals and thus stills quickly mushroomed in various parts of the country. As one might expect, the consumption of gin amongst the population skyrocketed as a result; and according to historian Iain Gately by 1723, 'every man, woman, and child in London knocked back more than a pint of gin per head per week'.[4] The effect on the population was dire, particularly in the city of London where squalid and decayed living conditions already made life difficult for many.

With time the government eventually noticed that overconsumption of gin among the population was not a force for good, and through five different Acts placed in 1729, 1736, 1743, 1747 and 1751, the authorities sought to bring matters under control.

In the time leading up to the Act of 1751 English painter, social critic and editorial cartoonist William Hogarth got involved in the fight against gin and he famously produced two engravings: *Gin Lane* and *Beer Street* with the intention of showing the madness of gin-induced dipsomania by

3 See H. P. Lovecraft, 'Anglo-Saxondom', in *Collected Essays Volume 5: Philosophy, Autobiography & Miscellany*, S. T. Joshi, ed. (New York: Hippocampus Press, 2006), 32–33.

4 Iain Gately, *Drink a Cultural History of Alcohol* (Gotham Books, 2008), 181. The alcohol per volume (APV) of gin ranges between 37.5 per cent and 50 per cent and in eighteenth-century England it was usually served by the dram or drachma, which measures 1/8 of an ounce. The high AVP of gin and because it was cheap to produce contributed to its popularity. To put it bluntly it was an easy and inexpensive way of getting drunk fast. It is possible that gin, a clear juniper flavoured spirit distilled from grain and malt was invented in seventeenth-century Holland. Etymologically speaking this makes sense because the word 'gin' derived from the older 'genever' or 'jenever' refers to juniper in the Dutch language.

contrasting it with the happy state of being of the 'healthy' beer drinker (see Figure 3.1 & 3.2).

Figure 3.1. William Hogarth, *Gin Lane* (1751). The engraving together with the accompanying verses is meant to shock and conveys human degradation to an extreme degree.

Figure 3.2. William Hogarth, *Beer Street* (1751). The engraving is a celebration of English industriousness and serves as an approval of having a pint of beer (or more) post-work hours. *Beer Street* comes in two versions. The first, which is depicted here, features a blacksmith lifting a Frenchman with one hand. The 1957 version replaced the Frenchman with a lump of meat and added a paviour and a maid.

Gin Lane is particularly disturbing because amidst the chaotic scenery that includes an impaled child, a child being fed gin and a hanged man we find 'Lady Gin' sitting on a staircase with her clothing in disarray exhibiting foul leg ulcers.[5] Furthermore, in her seemingly happy and careless daze, she lets her child plunge to its death over the nearby railing. The link to the terrible consequences of overconsumption of gin is clear and is further amplified upon noticing that the child of Lady Gin will meet its end at the front door of a basement gin store named 'Gin Royale' advertising its intoxicating beverages with the catchphrase: 'Drunk for a Penny/Dead Drunk for Two Pence/Clean Straw for Nothing'.

Both engravings originally came with accompanying verses, so none were to be mistaken about their individual messages. *Gin Lane* opens with the negative line: 'Gin, cursed Fiend, with Fury fraught' and Beer Street with the positive: 'Beer, happy Produce of our Isle'.

The Gin-Craze eventually faded away, but this singular episode in English history owes its end not only to governmental Acts and the dramatic engravings of a skilled artist. New ideas flourished in political philosophy addressing how society moulds people, and they likewise contributed to the effect. Romantic philosopher Jean-Jacques Rousseau's *The Social Contract* is important in this regard as it opens with the now famous line: 'Man is born free, and he is everywhere in chains.'[6] If we view the gin-craze personified by the gin-soaked hussy depicted in Hogarth's *Gin Street* through Rousseau's spectacles, it becomes clear that the drunken citizens of London may not solely be responsible for their fate. Their unfortunate situation could at least in part have been brought about by unfavourable social structures in eighteenth-century England. No doubt times were hard and particularly so for women, who were viewed as subordinate to men and who had little access to education and suffered from unfair laws that favoured men in matters concerning money and inheritance.

Overconsumption of alcohol remained a problem in England post the Gin-graze, but as we move into the nineteenth century, the problematic

5 The leg ulcers could be the result of syphilis, a venereal disease that could well have been introduced into Europe by sailors accompanying Christopher Columbus on his voyages to the New World. If the sores indeed are syphilitic leg ulcers it points to the promiscuity of Lady Gin and the possibility of her being a prostitute, which adds to the overall uneasiness of the engraving.

6 Jean-Jacques Rousseau, *The Social Contract*, Maurice Cranston, trans. (London: Penguin Books, 1968), 49.

custom was addressed from a different angle. Thomas Trotter, MD, and late physician to his Majesty's fleet under the command of Admiral Earl Howe, K. G.[7] alerted people to the dangers of alcohol from a medical perspective. Printed in London in 1804 Trotter's *An Essay, Medical, Philosophical, and Chemical on Drunkenness and Its Effect on the Human Body* leaves few in doubt that alcohol is a bad thing. He sets the tone already from the beginning on the title page with a quotation from Shakespeare's Othello: 'O! thou invisible spirit of wine, if thou hast no name to be known by, let us call thee – devil' and goes on not only to spell out the negative impact alcohol has on the human body but also how it wreaks havoc on the mind.[8] In italics Trotter writes: 'The habit of drunkenness is a disease of the mind.'[9]

The nineteenth century also saw the birth of teetotalism in England. The neologism refers to the total abstinence from alcoholic beverages, but how this rather peculiar name came about is unclear. A popular notion is that the term was coined quite unintentionally in 1833. The Charleston Observer notes:

> *Teetotalers*. – The origin of this convenient word, (as convenient almost, although not so general in its application as *loafer*,) is, we imagine, known but to few who use it. It originated, as we learn from the Landmark, with a man named Turner, a member of the Preston Temperance Society, who, having an impediment of speech, in addressing a meeting remarked, that partial abstinence from intoxicating liquors would not do; they must insist upon tee-tee- (stammering) tee total abstinence. Hence total abstainers have been called *teetotalers*.[10]

If the Charleston Observer is correct the curious word 'teetotaller' was born from the stuttering of Richard Turner – a member of the Preston Temperance Society founded in Preston, England in 1833 by local

7 K. G. refers to Knight of the Order of the Garter, which is an order of chivalry founded by King Edward III in 1348.

8 See William Shakespeare, 'Othello', in *Tragedies Volume 1* (London: Everyman's Library, 1992), II.iii, 280–282.

9 Thomas Trotter, *An Essay, Medical, Philosophical, and Chemical on Drunkenness and Its Effect on the Human Body* (London: Printed for T. N. Longman, and O. Rees, 1804). <https://wellcomecollection.org/works/bmkxze8z/items?canvas=9>, accessed 21 August 2023, 172.

10 *The Charleston Observer* 10, no. 44 (29 October 1836), 174, columns 4–5.

newspaper owner, industrialist and politician Joseph Livesey.[11] This singular society organised various meetings to promote their course and attract new members and in 1834 it founded the first ever temperance magazine *The Preston Temperance Advocate* that ran until 1837.

Bacchus in America

That the populace of America also came face to face with the joys and sorrows of alcohol is not surprising because many of the early European settlers were jovial drinkers.

After the American Revolution (1765–1783), whiskey became the national drink in America. It was a cheap and 'safe' drink since the alcohol eradicated germs and by the 1820s the average white American male downed about half a pint of whiskey per day.[12] However, the 'whiskey-craze' did not go unnoticed and medical doctors such as Benjamin Rush eventually began to speak up about the dark side of alcohol including the build-up of tolerance and the need for an increased intake over time if the desired euphoric state of mind were to be achieved.

Already in 1784 Rush published *An Inquiry into the Effects of Spirituous Liquors* and by 1850 it had reached massive popularity and sold a staggering 170,000 copies.[13] Rush argued that not only was alcohol dangerous to human health but also American democracy would suffer and ultimately break down if voters were nothing but drunken bacchants. Unemployment, crime, poverty, family violence, starvation, gambling and prostitution were, in Rush's view, associated with drunkenness and altogether it made for bad voters.

11 According to historian Iain Gately Turner's first name is Richard. See Gately, *Drink a Cultural History of Alcohol*, 273.

12 See W. J. Rorabaugh, *Prohibition: A Concise History* (Oxford: Oxford University Press, 2018), 7. The APV of whiskey was at the time about 50 per cent.

13 Ibid.

Rush was not the only physician battling against the consumption of alcohol in America. In 1812 the Massachusetts Society for the Suppression of Intemperance (MSSI) comprised members of the congregational clergy connected to the Andover Seminary; Boston business leaders and several physicians were founded. The society campaigned against the overconsumption of whiskey and represented a classical approach to temperance, meaning that temperance is about moderation and is something to be sought between two monsters – two extremes: too little and too much. To understand this better it is prudent to evoke the ancient Greek philosopher Aristotle who if he were alive today would argue that the raison d'être of the MSSI was to spread the idea that drinking alcohol is easy but to drink with the right person(s) and to the right degree and in the right time and for the right purpose and in the right way – that is not within everybody's power and is not easy and thus praiseworthy.[14]

However, among those involved in the fight against drunkenness, this particular attitude towards temperance was soon to give way to a more radical take on the matter. The American Temperance Society (ATS) founded in 1826 in Boston, Massachusetts together with religious groups including the Quakers, the Methodists and the Baptists were soon to denounce the call for temperance issued by MSSI and required members to take *the teetotal pledge* and keep away from all forms of alcohol. With time this particular approach to temperance gained influence and by 1842 the first law aimed at limiting the sale of alcohol in saloons had been put in place.[15]

Between 1840 and 1850 more than two million whiskey-drinking Irishmen and beer-loving Germans immigrated to America supplying as it were fresh support for the cult of Bacchus.[16] However, many an

14 Aristotle, *The Nichomachean Ethics*, H. Rackham, trans., Loeb Classical Library (Cambridge, MA: Harvard University Press, 2003), II. Ix. 2.

15 See Rorabaugh, *Prohibition: A Concise History*, 11–13.

16 The cult of Bacchus was an orgiastic cult originally meant for women only that expanded in Italy approximately 200 years BCE. Dionysus, the Greek God of wine and ecstasy, which the Romans labelled Bacchus, was the focal point of the cult. I take a modern follower of Bacchus to be a person who does not shy away from enjoyment and revelry involving drunkenness.

evangelical lobbied successfully for state-wide prohibition which was put into effect between 1851 and 1855 in the six states of New England, New York, Michigan, Indiana, Iowa and Delaware.[17] None of these laws lasted beyond 1865, the year the American Civil War ended but nonetheless a 'dry' movement had taken root and was gaining popularity. The movement turned into a cultural force with the advent of the Independent Order of Good Templars (IOGT) in 1851. Standing in opposition to alcohol-drinking Freemasons this lodge counted post-1865 seven million women and men as members.[18]

The following period ending with the eighteenth amendment to the United States Constitution in 1919, which saw a national ban on the production, importation, transportation and sale of alcoholic beverages represents a 'war' of attitudes. It was a clash between teetotalism and liberty.

A figure important to the general temperance movement is its foremost orator, John Bartholomew Gough (1817– 1886 (see Figure 3.3)).[19] His crusade against alcohol was felt considerably in both England and America and in 1880, ten years before Lovecraft was born, he published *Sunlight and Shadow,* a book containing many a dramatic proclamation, including that beer is the most animalising of drinks and a beverage that dulls the intellect, clouds the moral sense and 'feeds the sensual and beastly nature' in us.[20]

17 Ibid., 21.

18 Ibid., 20.

19 Gough died while lecturing and is buried at Hope Cemetery in Worchester, MA.

20 Gough, John Bartholomew Gough, *Sunlight and Shadow or Learnings from My Life-Work* (London: Hodder and Stoughton, 1880), 364.

Figure 3.3. John Bartholomew Gough (1817–1886).

Although Prohibition produced positive effects among the population, including a dramatic decline in cases of cirrhosis of the liver and the number of arrests due to drunkenness, it lost its appeal over time.[21] One problem was that the law by and large was draconian in nature and violators faced heavy fines, imprisonment and confiscation of property. Additionally, it took an army of government agents, also known as G-men, with intrusive powers to enforce the amendment and it gave

21 See Robert J. MacCoun & P. Reuter, *Drug War Heresies: Learning from Other Vices, Times, and Places* (Cambridge: Cambridge University Press, 2001), 161.

birth to new kinds of criminals including bootleggers, moonshiners and rumrunners.[22]

Championed by Franklin Roosevelt, the twenty-first amendment to the American constitution put an end to Prohibition in 1932 but the repeal did not signal a total victory of 'wet' over 'dry'. Individual teetotallers as well as dry communities dedicated to Prohibition lived on and exist in America even today and thus it can be said that the war of attitudes never really ended.

In Vino Veritas: The Early Lovecraft (1890–1925)

Lovecraft was exposed to this war of attitudes quite early in life. At the age of 5 or 6, Lovecraft supposedly read Gough's *Sunlight and Shadow,* which the Phillips family had a copy of in the family library.[23] Whether he picked it up by his own initiative or per recommendation is uncertain, but one can speculate that because his beloved grandfather Whipple van Buren Phillips spent time in the temperance town of Delavan, Illinois in the 1850s it is quite possible that Lovecraft was introduced to Gough's book by his grandfather.[24]

That grandfather Phillips influenced the young Lovecraft on matters of alcohol could explain why Lovecraft, in a letter from 13 February 1928,

22 Bootleggers were smugglers who during Prohibition continued to sell alcohol. The term originates in the time of King George III where smugglers hid goods in their voluminous sea-boots to avoid the attention of the king's guard. Moonshiners produced low quality alcohol in secret during the prohibition period. The term is akin to the English term moonraker, which refers to mid-sixteenth-century smugglers in Wiltshire, a county in southwest England. Rumrunners were international bootleggers that during prohibition traded in quality mainly between the Caribbean islands and America. One of the more famous rumrunners is William S. McCoy who smuggled Scotch (whiskey from Scotland) into Georgia on board his schooner *Henry L. Marshall* registered under the British flag.

23 See Lovecraft's 1916 letter to Reinhardt Kleiner in Lovecraft, *Selected Letters I 1911–1924*, 35.

24 S. T. Joshi, *I am Providence: The Life and Times of H. P. Lovecraft*, vol. 1 (New York: Hippocampus Press, 2010), 6.

proclaims that wine has been banished in his family for three generations.[25] This is a remarkable statement and if it is true, how could Lovecraft possibly have such knowledge of his family, unless a thoughtful family member, like Whipple van Buren Phillips, handed it to him?[26]

That Lovecraft took issue with the consumption of alcohol is evident from several of his early philosophical writings. To add some weight to this claim, let us begin by looking at Lovecraft's own amateur magazine *The Conservative* that ran for thirteen issues between 1915 and 1923. In the first issue Lovecraft placed an editorial stating that: 'The Conservative will ever be found an enthusiastic champion of total abstinence and prohibition.'[27] It is hard to imagine a clearer statement linking *The Conservative* with teetotalism without the actual use of the word. The piece finishes with Lovecraft reminding his fellow conservatives that 'he who strives against the Hydra-monster Rum, strives most to conserve his fellow man.'[28] Now 'Hydra-monster Rum' is a negative moniker for rum, and it seems safe to say that Lovecraft uses this phrase as a generic reference to what he perceived as one of the many scourges of alcohol.

The editorial is followed in subsequent issues by a series of essays or heated opinion pieces rallying against alcohol starting with 'Liquor and its friends' that appeared in *The Conservative* 1, No. 3, October 1915. Here, Lovecraft protests the reinstatement of the presence of liquor at American State dinners by new secretary of state Robert Lansing, who took over from William Jennings Bryan. Bryan, a religious fundamentalist, pacifist and supporter of Prohibition, managed to abolish wine from tables of the state and thus in Lovecraft's view gave

25 See H. P. Lovecraft, *The Spirit of Revision: Lovecraft's Letters to Zealia Brown Reed Bishop*, Sean Branney & Andrew Leman, eds (HPLHS, 2015), 104–105.

26 Although it might be that alcohol had not been a part of the Lovecraft family for three generations, one source speaks of Lovecraft being intoxicated by alcohol at least once in his life. The story goes that Lovecraft attended a party where his drink was supposedly spiked by a roommate of Samuel Loveman called Pat McGrath with the result that Lovecraft became talkative, smiling, laughing and gesticulating. See Samuel Loveman, 'Lovecraft as a Conversationalist', in *Lovecraft Remembered*, Peter Cannon, ed. (Sauk City, WI: Arkham House Publishers, 1998), 211.

27 See H. P. Lovecraft, 'Editorial', in *Collected Essays Volume 1: Amateur Journalism*, S. T. Joshi, ed. (New York: Hippocampus Press, 2004), 51.

28 Ibid.

'the American people a high governmental example of decency'.[29] Nevertheless, he resigned from his post after the torpedoing of Ocean liner *Lusitania* by a German U-boat in May 1915.[30] Lovecraft finishes the essay by making clear that those who are not on his side in matters of alcohol disregard natural law and moral rectitude and will contribute to the downfall of civilisation.[31]

'More Chain Lightning' appeared in *United Official Quarterly* 2, No. 1 in October 1915.[32] It celebrates amateur journalist and editor of the journal *Chain Lightning* Andrew Francis Lockhart who had successfully campaigned for the closing of licensed saloons in the city of Milbank. Central to the piece is Lovecraft's pro-prohibitionist argument stating:

> As to the 'personal liberty', 'rights of man', and other popular phrases similarly misused, there are few indeed who can fail to perceive that the 'liberty' and 'right' of a man voluntary to transform himself to a beast, and in the end to degrade himself and his descendants permanently in the scale of evolution, is equivalent to his 'liberty' and 'right' to rob and murder at will. If the law may justly suppress theft and homicide, it may certainly with equal justice suppress the manufacture, sale and consumption of that liquid evil which incites most of the world's theft and homicide. As to 'moderate drinking', we might on similar ethics condone 'moderate larceny' or 'moderate manslaughter'. Human nature admits of no exact middle course in drinking. He who usually drinks 'a little', will always on occasion drink 'a little too much', wherefore the only sane course is absolutely total abstinence.[33]

Lovecraft's argument is overly dramatic and much too extreme. Admittedly alcohol influences a person's cognitive functions and sometimes quite negatively, but to enjoy a drink of one's own free volition does not usually result in

29 See H. P. Lovecraft, 'Editorial', in *Collected Essays Volume 5: Philosophy, Autobiography & Miscellany*, S. T. Joshi, ed. (New York: Hippocampus Press, 2006), 16.

30 For more information on how the sinking of Lusitania inspired Lovecraft and in particular his short story 'The Temple' (1920) see Géza A. G. Reilly, '"All Things Are Noble Which Serve the German State": Nationalism in Lovecraft's "The Temple"', in *Lovecraft Annual No. 11*, S. T. Joshi, ed. (New York: Hippocampus Press, 2017).

31 See Lovecraft, 'Editorial', 16–17.

32 Chain lightning is a slang word for raw whiskey, that is, whiskey in no need of maturation.

33 See H. P. Lovecraft, 'More Chain Lightning', in *Collected Essays Volume 5: Philosophy, Autobiography & Miscellany*, S. T. Joshi, ed. (New York: Hippocampus Press, 2006), 18–19.

endless bacchanal and to equate moderate drinking with moderate larceny or moderate manslaughter in order to persuade the reader of the beauty of teetotalism is more telling of Lovecraft's disgust for alcohol than it bears witness to good argumentation.[34]

'A Remarkable Document' appeared in the *Conservative* 3, No. 1, July 1917 and is less pompous than Lovecraft's previous writing on the demon rum. It praises the temperance advocate Booth Tarkington who, instead of relying on lofty idealism, approached temperance and Prohibition from a scientific angle. At this point, a beginning sophistication of Lovecraft's attitude towards alcohol is emerging and we also get a hint of Lovecraft's boredom with the ordinary, which comes to light in his 1917 poem 'Fact and Fancy' and later becomes an important theme in his wonder stories. Lovecraft writes:

> No one can deny that life in conventionally civilised communities is dull and monotonous to the point of loathsomeness; and if this basic ennui be so potent a factor in the desire for liquor, then we cannot expect to banish the evil till we have found some means of brightening the gloom which causes it.[35]

In this statement Lovecraft, metaphorically speaking, puts on Rousseau's spectacles and connects with the 'victims of alcohol' by recognising that they have a common enemy, namely the dullness of everyday life. Lovecraft speculates that in order to do away with the plague of liquor one has to take care of ennui first and this somewhat practical if not Romantic approach is new.

'The Recognition of Temperance' is the last philosophical essay evidencing Lovecraft's views on matters of alcohol that I will focus on here. Published in *Little Budget of Knowledge and Nonsense* 1, No. 1 in April 1917, this short piece celebrates the notion that science has caught up with the drinkers and that prohibition is spreading steadily in Europe and America based on the recognition

34 For more information on Lovecraft's aversion towards ecstasy, revelry and the cultist rites associated with Bacchus, see Dennis Quinn, 'Endless Bacchanal: Rome, Livy and Lovecraft's Cthulhu Cult', in *Lovecraft Annual No. 5*, S. T. Joshi, ed. (New York: Hippocampus Press, 2011).

35 See H. P. Lovecraft, 'A Remarkable Document', in *Collected Essays Volume 5: Philosophy, Autobiography & Miscellany*, S. T. Joshi, ed. (New York: Hippocampus Press, 2006), 26.

of 'alcohol as foe of national efficiency and prosperity'.[36] The wording of the essay is sober and somewhat bereft of the drama Lovecraft evoked in 'Liquor and Its Friends' as the emphasis is on the transformation of the Temperance Movement, its move away from evangelism and moralisation and its embrace of science and government. However, it also delivers a criticism of the supposed cultivated upper middle-class cosmopolitan whose wine cellar still celebrates the essential evil. 'The presence of liquor on the sideboards of a certain type of "solid citizen" is as distressing as it is incongruous', Lovecraft writes.[37] The essay ends on a positive note stating that alcohol, the 'mother of ruin and death' is now exposed for what it is, and that the 'social prestige of wine' must be destroyed through 'lofty example and polite ridicule'.[38]

Young Lovecraft's formidable aversion towards alcohol is made quite clear from reading his early poetry. In 'The Power of Wine: A Satire' (1914) Lovecraft writes:

> Unhappy man above the beasts was plac'd;
>
> Stript of his joys, and with mere Reason grac'd:
>
> Sweet Wine alone his pleasures can restore;
>
> Let him but quaff, and he's a beast once more![39]

The satirical element of the poem is obvious as Lovecraft portrays the unfortunate predicament of human beings. Unlike the other beasts of nature, human beings are endowed with the ability to have reasons for action, but rational deliberation often entails awareness of complexities, not forgetting doubt, and thus trouble and unhappiness enter human life. Owing to its ability to dull the faculties, the restoration of happiness is found in the

36 See H. P. Lovecraft, 'The Recognition of Temperance', in *Collected Essays Volume 5: Philosophy, Autobiography & Miscellany*, S. T. Joshi, ed. (New York: Hippocampus Press, 2006), 284.

37 Ibid.

38 Ibid.

39 H. P. Lovecraft, 'The Power of Wine: A Satire', in *The Ancient Track: The Complete Poetical Works of H. P. Lovecraft*, S. T. Joshi, ed. (New York: Hippocampus press, 2013), 212–213.

consumption of wine that effectively levels the consumer of alcohol with the non-rational beasts on the *scala naturae*.[40]

By paying attention to the somewhat spiteful wording of the poem it is clear that they parallel in tone and suggestion those of John Bartholomew Gough, who acrimoniously promoted the idea that alcoholic beverages dull the intellect and calls forth the beast in us.

The young Lovecraft was quite aware that his teetotalism was not merely a personal idiosyncrasy and that he was part of a potentially revolutionary movement aiming to straighten a wayward nation. He did not shy away from taking leadership, which the first stanza of *Temperance Song* from 1916 stands in support of:

We are a band of brothers
We fight the demon Rum,
With all our strength until at length
A better time shall come.
(Chorus)
Hurrah Hurrah! for Temperance, Hurrah!
'Tis sweet to think that deadly drink
Some day no more shall mar![41]

For Lovecraft to use the phrase 'band of brothers' originating in the famous St Crispin's Day speech from Shakespeare's *Henry V* indicates an attempt to call up epic feelings in his fellow teetotallers – feelings

40 *Scala naturae* is the Latin word for 'ladder of being' which is a concept derived from the writings of the ancient Greek philosophers particularly Aristotle who organises life hierarchically in accordance with level of perfection. Human beings are the most perfect, followed by animals, plants and minerals at the bottom of the scale. Christian scholars in the medieval period added God and angelic beings above human beings.

41 H. P. Lovecraft, 'Temperance Song', in *The Ancient Track: The Complete Poetical Works of H. P. Lovecraft*, S. T. Joshi, ed. (New York: Hippocampus Press, 2013), 397–398.

signalling that by rallying together and walk that extra mile in the name of teetotalism, victory over the demon rum would be within reach.

Going forward to the year 1919 Lovecraft displays his poetic splendour once more by producing two satirical poems hailing the downfall of Bacchus in America and the success of the temperance movement. The short 'On Prohibition' (1919) claiming 'the Demon Rum is dying' is one of them and 'Monody on the Late King Alcohol' (1919) where Lovecraft has the Maenads – the maniacal dancing Dionysus worshippers from Greek mythology exclaim '*Alcohol* is dead' is the other.[42]

The year 1919 signals a turning point for Lovecraft because from this year onwards no poetry of his is concerned with temperance and prohibition. However, things are different when it comes to fiction.

Figure 3.4. Les Edwards, *The Necronomicon: Tomb,* 2007. Courtesy of Les Edwards.

42 H. P. Lovecraft, '"On Prohibition" & Monody on the Late King Alcohol', in *The Ancient Track: The Complete Poetical Works of H. P. Lovecraft*, S. T. Joshi, ed. (New York: Hippocampus Press, 2013), 243.

The macabre tale 'The Tomb' was written in June 1917 and later published in the March 1922 edition of *The Vagrant* (see Figure 3.4). It tells the story of the eccentric and alienated Jervas Dudley who finds an old tomb in a wooded hollow close to home, harbouring the remains of the Hyde family. The story is important because it contains a rather morose '*memento mori/carpe diem*' orientated drinking song of which the first two stanzas read:[43]

> The Tomb. Come hither, my lads, with your tankards of ale,
> And drink to the present before it shall fail;
> Pile each on your platter a mountain of beef,
> For 'tis eating and drinking that bring us relief:
> So fill up your glass,
> For life will soon pass;
> When you're dead ye'll ne'er drink to your king or your lass!
>
> The Tomb: Anacreon had a red nose, so they say;
> But what's a red nose if ye're happy and gay?
> Gad split me! I'd rather be red whilst I'm here,
> Than white as a lily –and dead half a year!
> So Betty, my miss,
> Come give me a kiss;
> In hell there's no innkeeper's daughter like this![44]

The Drinking Song reveals one of the unsettling problems with human existence – namely, that each one of us lives on borrowed time – but it also teaches us how to deal with this singular problem. The song promotes a hedonistic philosophy but where the first stanza hails the somewhat Ecclesiastical idiom: 'eat, drink and be merry' the second with its celebration of Betty adds a sexual dimension to the supposed wisdom of

43 'Memento mori' is Latin for 'remember that you will die'. The origin of the phase is uncertain but philosophical deliberation on human mortality goes back as far as antiquity where Plato voices it in the *Phaedo*, 64a4. The aphorism 'Carpe Diem' translates 'seize the day' and originates in the writing of the Roman poet Horace. See Horace, *Odes and Epodes*, Niall Rudd, ed. and trans., Loeb Classical Library (Cambridge: Cambridge University Press, 2004), 1.11.8.

44 H. P. Lovecraft, 'The Tomb', in *The New Annotated H. P. Lovecraft: Beyond Arkham*, Leslie S. Klinger, ed. (New York: Liveright Publishing Corporation, 2019), 3–14.

Solomon, transmuting it into a more Dashwoodian outlook rooted in the motto 'do what thou wilt'.[45] At first glance this might seem an over-interpretation, but the extent of Dudley's drunken revelry at the Hyde family's mansion later in the story indicates otherwise. Here Dudley confesses to the reader: 'Amidst a wild and reckless throng I was the wildest and most abandoned. Gay blasphemy poured in torrents from my lips, and in my shocking sallies I heeded no law of God, Man, or Nature.'[46] What happens to Dudley in this Hellfire-Club-ish setting is the very animalisation Gough warns about in his book *Sunlight and Shadow* and what Lovecraft wished to convey with his use of the word 'beast' in the poem *The Power of Wine*. Dudley is a bacchanal supreme, and his drunken revelry leads to an eroticised state utterly repugnant to Lovecraft who

45 Shaped as a response to the question of how to live, the part of the Old Testament labelled 'Ecclesiastes' or in Hebrew 'Qohelet', meaning teacher or preacher, contains philosophical idioms such as 'eat, drink and be merry' (Ecclesiastes, 8:15). The author of the idioms is unknown, but scholars have thought it to be the legendary, wise and incredibly wealthy King Solomon. Solomon was king of Israel supposedly around 970–931 BC and according to legend he processed a magic ring called the Seal of Solomon that enabled him to command demons or Jinn.

Other responses to the question of how to live also exist in the philosophical literature. The Ancient Greek philosopher Aristotle, for example, suggests that we should live a 'eudaimonic life' and distance ourselves from the life of pleasure. See Aristotle, *The Nicomachean Ethics*, H. Rackham, trans., Loeb Classical Library (Cambridge, MA: Harvard University Press, 2003) and for the Roman stoic philosopher Seneca life was to be owned; to be about accomplishment and not to be wasted on 'wine and lust'. See Seneca, 'On the Shortness of Life', in *Moral Essays*, vol. II, John W. Basore, trans., Loeb Classical Library (Cambridge, MA: Harvard University Press, 1933), I. 3, VII, 1.

Sir Francis Dashwood or simply Lord Dashwood is associated with the hedonistic orientated hell-fire clubs in eighteenth-century Britain. The clubs are surrounded by mystery, and in what capacity Dashwood was involved is uncertain but he is rightly associated with a group of people called the Medmenham Friars which in popular imagination has become the Hell-Fire Club. The club lived by the motto: 'Fay ce que vouldras' or 'Do what you will' and serves as a place where rich and powerful people could engage in 'immoral behaviour' and revelry in accord with that of the ancient cult of Bacchus. See Evelyn Lord, *The Hell-Fire Clubs: Sex, Satanism and Secret Societies* (New Haven, CT: Yale University Press, 2008), 98.

46 Lovecraft, 'The Tomb', 11.

believed 'eroticism belongs to a lower order of instincts and is an animal rather than nobly human quality'.[47]

Two years after writing 'The Tomb' Lovecraft produced the short story 'Old Bugs' (1919). Published in *The Shuttered Room and Other Pieces* by Arkham House in 1959, its purpose was to dissuade Alfred Galpin, a friend of Lovecraft's, from sampling alcohol before it became prohibited. We know this because in his 'Memories of Grandpa Theobald'; Lovecraft's favourite nom de plume at the time, Galpin writes:

On the occasion of Prohibition I sallied forth to find out what the stuff was like before it was banned, told him of the results and received in admonition a farcically diverting skit in which he indulged to the utmost his passion for slang.[48]

The farcically diverting skit that Galpin is referring to is indeed 'Old Bugs'. Set in the 1950s the story is centred on Sheehan's Pool Room, the acknowledged centre to Chicago's subterranean traffic in liquor and narcotics and the titular character Old Bugs, who is no other than the future Alfred Galpin himself, brought to an unbearable low point by 'evil habits, dating from a first drink taken years before in woodland seclusion'.[49] In an introductory note to the first publication of 'Old Bugs', Galpin states that in the end of the story Lovecraft had addressed him and asked, '*Now* will you be good?!' adding a further authoritative rhetorical punch to an otherwise emotional tour de force.[50]

The short story 'Sweet Ermengarde or the Heart of a Country Girl' originally written between 1919 and 1921 under the pseudonym of Percy Simple and published in 1943 in Arkham House's *Beyond the Wall of Sleep* likewise testifies to Lovecraft's continuing preoccupation with alcohol. The first paragraph of 'chapter I: A Simple Rustic Maid' reads:

47 See Lovecraft's 1920 letter to Reinhardt Kleiner in Lovecraft, *Selected Letters I 1911–1924*, 106.

48 Alfred Galpin, 'Memories of a Friendship', in *Lovecraft Remembered*, Peter Cannon, ed. (Sauk City, WI, 1998), 165.

49 H. P. Lovecraft, 'Old Bugs', *The H. P. Lovecraft Archive*, <http://www.hplovecraft.com/writings/texts/fiction/ob.aspx>, accessed 21 August 2013.

50 Joshi & Schultz, *An H. P. Lovecraft Encyclopedia*, 193.

> Ermengarde Stubbs was the beauteous blonde daughter of Hiram Stubbs, a poor but honest farmer-bootlegger of Hogton, Vt. Her name was originally Ethyl Ermengarde, but her father persuaded her to drop the praenomen after the passage of the 18th Amendment, averring that it made him thirsty by reminding him of ethyl alcohol, C_2H_5OH. His own products contained mostly methyl or wood alcohol, CH_3OH.[51]

Besides bearing witness to Lovecraft's comical acumen and affection for chemistry the paragraph hints at the ruinous lineage of sweet Ermengarde. The idea is that her connection to the honest bootlegger Hiram Stubbs is corruptive due to his intercourse with alcohol and plays to her selfish and most manipulative behaviour at the end of the story.

The final work from Lovecraft's earlier writing that incorporates a warning against alcohol is 'The Quest of Iranon'. Written in 1921 and published in the *Galleon* in 1935, this dreamland story centres on Iranon, a yellow-haired youthful singer who claims he is a prince hailing from Aira, a city of unheard beauty. Iranon is a wanderer and his preferences contrast those of the dromedary-men in the story, who in their drunken and ribald habitués mirror the exploits of the Hyde families and their guests in Lovecraft's 'The Tomb'.

During his quest, Iranon teams up with the boy Romnod, a fellow seeker of beauty and song, and together they travel to Oonai, the city of lutes and dancing where they dwell until Romnod dies as an old, dream-deprived alcoholic. Iranon, a teetotaller and thus untouched by the ruinous powers of wine, remains young and finally leaves Oonai to continue his quest for Aira only ultimately to fail because Aira is a utopia, a place that does not exist.

The emphasis on the harmful effects of wine is clear enough in this little Dunsanian masterpiece, but unlike in Lovecraft's earlier writing, the atmosphere the dreamer of Providence builds around the drunken is one of sadness. Alcohol in Lovecraft's view deprives human beings of the finer and more sensitive qualities upon which the dreamer and poet depend.

51 H. P. Lovecraft, 'Sweet Ermengarde or the Heart of a Country Girl', *The H. P. Lovecraft Archive*, <http://www.hplovecraft.com/writings/texts/fiction/se.aspx>, accessed 21 August 2023.

In Aqua Sanitas: The Later Lovecraft (1925–1937)

On the 3rd of March 1924, Lovecraft married Sonia Greene whom he had met at an amateur journalist convention and soon moved in with her in her apartment in Brooklyn, New York. Things were great at first, but when Sonia lost her business and Lovecraft found himself unemployable financial trouble quickly turned life sour for the newlyweds. Sonia and Lovecraft eventually separated and in April 1926 Lovecraft moved back to Providence.

The year 1926 signals a turning point in Lovecraft's authorship because during August and September he produced his signature piece of fiction 'The Call of Cthulhu'. Published in *Weird Tales* in 1928, the novelette deals in part with the infamous Cthulhu cult, whose members share many of the characteristics attributed to the intoxicated maenad or bacchant of ancient times. The nameless rites and bloodthirstiness of the degenerate cult of Esquimaux that Professor William Channing Webb speaks of at the American Archaeological Society's annual get-together in St Louis testifiy to this.[52] Inspector Legrasse tale of the murdering Louisiana swamp worshippers whose animal fury and orgiastic licence elevated them to daemoniac heights is likewise indicative. Perhaps the strongest support in favour of the Cthulhu cultists' commonality with the cult of Bacchus is the description of what will happen once great Cthulhu emerges from his tomb to revive his subjects. By then humankind would be:

> Free and wild and beyond good and evil, with laws and morals thrown aside and all men shouting and killing and revelling in joy. Then the liberated Old Ones would teach them new ways to shout and kill and revel and enjoy

52 Lovecraft uses the term 'esquimaux' (French for eskimo meaning either (1) 'eater of raw meat', (2) *excommunicati* or excommunicated ones, i.e. non-Christian or (3) one who nets snowshoes) in *The Call of Cthulhu* but today the designation is highly discussed and by some deemed antiquated. In Canada and Greenland, the term 'Inuit' is preferred by the indigenous people but in Alaska this term is insufficient as it does not cover the Yupik-people. The word 'Inuit' simply does not exist in their language.

> themselves, and all the earth would flame with a holocaust of ecstasy and freedom.[53]

It is clear that the world will end in utter orgiastic madness. The bacchanal of all time equals the end of all things civil as humankind by then has surrendered to headlong hedonism and elevated individual pleasure to the point of ultimate value.

Lovecraft's use of the phrase 'beyond good and evil' signals a turning away from a traditional order and he borrowed the phrase from German philosopher Friedrich Nietzsche (1844–1900) who is one of the high priests and indeed victims of Romanticism.[54] Nietzsche, who like Lovecraft detested alcohol, is the author of *Beyond Good and Evil*, in which he criticises dogmatism, traditional philosophers and promotes a new philosophy based on free spirits whom he describes as 'investigators to the point of cruelty, with uninhibited fingers for the unfathomable, with teeth and stomachs for the most indigestible'.[55] This describes well the Cthulhu cultist, and both cultist and free spirit can rightfully be labelled Dionysian. However, to be a Nietzschean free spirit is not the same as being a revelling Cthulhu cultist. The Dionysian aspect of Nietzsche's philosophy emphasises creativity and a 'yes' to life, contrasting with that of 'Apollo worshipping' philosophers like Socrates, who effectively said 'no' to life and annihilated himself by drinking hemlock when sentenced to death by the city of Athens. Nietzsche's free spirit involves looking for greatness, autonomy and individuality. It is the business of creating new values while rebelling against the traditional ascetic ones. This is precisely what the Cthulhu cultist is doing, but the cultist is

53 H. P. Lovecraft, 'The Call of Cthulhu', in *The New Annotated H. P. Lovecraft*, Leslie S. Klinger, ed. (New York: Liveright Publishing Corporation, 2014), 142.

54 See Carl Schmitt, *Political Romanticism*, Guy Oakes, trans. (Cambridge, MA: MIT Press, 2011), 20.

55 See Friedrich Nietzsche, *Beyond Good and Evil*, Walter Kaufmann, trans. (New York: Vintage, 1989), §44. Nietzsche aversion towards alcohol is evident when reading his *Twilight of the Idols* where he holds that the 'The German people has deliberately made itself stupid, for nearly a millennium: nowhere have the two great European narcotics, alcohol and Christianity, been abused more dissolutely'. See Friedrich Nietzsche, *Afgudernes ragnarok*, Jens Erik Kristensen & Lars-Henrik Schmidt, trans. (Copenhagen: Gyldendal, 1999), 65.

not free to create new values. A Cthulhu cultist is at best liberated from old values but remains enthralled by hedonism dictated partly by the Old Ones. If truly free she would be able to do something else other than shout, kill and revel in joy but that is simply not the case. Armed with the teachings of the Old Ones, the cultist takes hedonism to a level indistinguishable from sadism, where civilisation is impossible, and that is anti-Nietzschean.

In the immediate aftermath of writing 'The Call of Cthulhu' Lovecraft sought to forge a connection between his works set in the dreamlands and what was later to be known as the Cthulhu Mythos and again alcohol was used as a plot device.

In the short story 'Pickman's model' (1926) we meet the hardboiled but unbalanced narrator Thurber who struggles to convey to his nephew Eliot the secrets of reality he has uncovered during his aesthetic exploits with the New England painter, Richard Upton Pickman. During the colloquy, Thurber reaches out for alcohol three times in order to calm his nerves, only finally in a display of Aristotelian moderation to call for coffee because as he puts it: 'We've had enough of the other stuff but I for one need something.'[56] The idea that alcohol can have a positive effect hints at a change in Lovecraft's attitude. This new outlook presents itself again in 1928, when Lovecraft learned that publisher Farnsworth Wright, who suffered from Parkinson's disease, on occasion drank too much. In a display of sympathy, Lovecraft contemplated sending him a case of 'synthetic bootleg brilliancy', that is, alcohol.[57]

That alcohol can be a force of good is also echoed in the 1927 novelette *The Case of Charles Dexter Ward,* where Lovecraft lets Doctor Willett

56 H. P. Lovecraft, 'Pickman's Model', in *The New Annotated H. P. Lovecraft: Beyond Arkham*, Leslie S. Klinger, ed. (New York: Liveright Publishing Corporation, 2019), 311–328.

57 L. Sprague de Camp, *H. P. Lovecraft: A Biography* (New York: Doubleday, 1975), 305. de Camp refers to a late September 1928 letter from Lovecraft to August Derleth, but unfortunately without stating precisely in which letter the passage is to be found.

regain consciousness with the aid of brandy after his horrifying experiences in the catacombs beneath Joseph Curwen's bungalow.[58]

Alcohol, as well as the ghoulish Pickman, plays a role in the wondrous dreamland novella *The Dream-Quest of Unknown Kadath*. Written between 1926 and 1927, but first published by Arkham House in 1943, it centres on Lovecraft's alter ego and dreamer extraordinaire, Randolf Carter who enters the Dreamlands on a quest to reach Kadath, the elusive dwelling place of the gods. During his quest Carter consults the Zoogs, who share with him their moon-wine which Carter wickedly makes use of later in the story when he questions the patriarch Atal in the Temple of the Elder Ones in Ulthar. Atal, being somewhat closemouthed, soon falls victim to Carter's moon-vine, and robbed of his reserve he 'babbles freely of forbidden things' thus propelling Carter onwards towards Ngranek on the isle of Oriab. However, at this point in time Lovecraft is back to his old teetotaller self and the 'dry' philosopher of Providence is quick to punish Carter for his wickedness and liaison with alcohol. In Dylath-Leen Carter tries his moon-wine trick yet again, but this time on a sinfully smirking merchant who remains unaffected. In a sinister act of quid pro quo, the merchant offers Carter a taste of his own wine, and Carter soon loses consciousness despite his exercise of temperance. He later wakes up surrounded by sardonic merchants on the deck of a ship flying with unusual swiftness on the coast of the Southern Sea.[59]

As we move into the last decade of Lovecraft's life, it is evident that he loses his faith in Prohibition. 'In 1919 I was a whole-hearted prohibitionist, but in 1928 I am more or less neutral,' Lovecraft writes in a letter to Zealia Bishop.[60] The reason for this change of attitude is grounded in

58 H. P. Lovecraft, 'The Case of Charles Dexter Ward', in *The New Annotated H. P. Lovecraft*, Leslie S. Klinger, ed. (New York: Liveright Publishing Corporation, 2014), 291.

59 H. P. Lovecraft, 'The Dream-quest of Unknown Kadath', in *The New Annotated H. P. Lovecraft: Beyond Arkham*, Leslie S. Klinger, ed. (New York: Liveright Publishing Corporation, 2019), 341–342.

60 See Lovecraft's letter dated 13 February 1928 to Zealia Brown Reed Bishop in *The Spirit of Revision: Lovecraft's Letters to Zealia Brown Reed Bishop*, Sean Branney & Andrew Leman, eds (HPLHS, 2015), 104–105.

the fact that despite the constitutional ban, alcohol was relatively easy to get hold of in 1928 and the social improvement Lovecraft previously thought outlawing alcohol would bring simply did not occur.

This widespread practice of bootlegging and the seemingly unquenchable thirst for alcohol amongst Americans found its way into Lovecraft's novel *The Case of Charles Dexter Ward*. Published in an abridged version in *Weird Tales* in 1941, the novel takes place in Rhode Island during the time of Prohibition and bootleggers make an entry in Chapter 3 where Sergt. Riley of the Second Station flags bootleggers as the likely culprits to acts of vandalism, including hole digging in and around The North Burial Ground.[61]

The everyday nature of crime related to alcohol is emphasised again later in the novel where Lovecraft has several 'hi-jackers' on a quest for liquor shipments shocked when uncovering human remains and not alcohol inside a number of coffins bound for wizard Curwen's bungalow.[62]

That Lovecraft was aware that spirits such as whiskey were easy to get hold of even in the lowliest of places during the time of Prohibition is evident when reading 'The Shadow over Innsmouth'. Here Lovecraft allows the narrator to purchase an easily obtainable but expensive quart bottle of whiskey in the rear of a dingy variety-store in Innsmouth. Echoing the methods of Randolf Carter, the purpose of this action is to get hold of the 'magic' that will loosen the tongue of the traumatised drunkard Zadok Allen and move the plot forward towards its dramatic conclusion.[63]

61 H. P. Lovecraft, 'The Case of Charles Dexter Ward', in *The New Annotated H. P. Lovecraft*, Leslie S. Klinger, ed. (New York: Liveright Publishing Corporation, 2014), 241.

62 Ibid., 253.

63 H. P. Lovecraft, 'The Shadow over Innsmouth', in *The New Annotated H. P. Lovecraft*, Leslie S. Klinger, ed. (New York: Liveright Publishing Corporation, 2014), 598.

Summary and Possibility: A Dry Philosopher in a New Light

Taking all into consideration there can be no doubt that Lovecraft was a dramatic teetotaller. This is evident from his early writing where his bombastic views in favour of total abstinence and Prohibition are akin to those of both Joseph Livesey and John Bartholomew Gough.

The later Lovecraft is somewhat more nuanced because the negative consequences of Prohibition became hard for him to ignore since he was concerned not merely with personal gentlemanly behaviour and civility but also society as a healthy orderly whole. If Prohibition did not work as a force of good, then he was quite ready to abandon it in his later years. Having said that, Lovecraft did not change his mind on alcohol itself, and his utter disgust for it never diminished. As stated in the beginning of the chapter it was an aesthetic matter to him and drinking was simply ugly.

However, evidence that Lovecraft changed his mind with regard to the presence of alcohol in society can be found in a 1932 letter addressed to American fantasy writer Robert E. Howard who famously created Conan the Barbarian and Solomon Kane and who enjoyed his beer immensely.[64] In here Lovecraft states that he can sympathise with those who are inclined to 'grant the hard-pressed classes the surcease to drink as a compensation for their burdens and helplessness'.[65] In doing so Lovecraft displays a keen awareness of the sufferings of others in a society far from perfect however supplying alcoholic beverages to the downtrodden was not Lovecraft's preferred method of helping out those in need. He continues:

> The more drink-sodden they get, the worse their biological stock becomes, and the less chance they have of getting out of their rut either by individual success or by conceded political action toward a more equitable social order. […] It would be wiser to study means for the reduction of general misery through the controlled allocation of labouring opportunities, the granting of old-age pensions and unemployment

64 Mark Finn, *Blood and Thunder* (Austin: MonkeyBrain Books, 2006), 93–94.

65 See H. P. Lovecraft's letter to Robert E. Howard in H. P. Lovecraft, *Selected Letters IV 1932–1934*, August Derleth & James Turner, eds (Sauk City, WI: Arkham House Publishers, 1976), 57–58.

> incurrence, and the gradual undermining of excess-profit motive, instead of condoning the woes of the helpless by giving them poison to make them forget about it.[66]

The first part of the citation makes it clear that although Lovecraft cares about the wellbeing of his fellow citizens he still entertains the idea that alcohol is corruptive. Alcohol might bring relief momentarily but in the long run the bad effects of drinking far outweigh the good. The latter part of the citation is indicative of Lovecraft's growing engagement with political philosophy and his inclination towards socialism, which he thought a possible remedy for bettering society.[67]

In some sense Lovecraft became a more balanced or temperate teetotaller in his later years. The forceful outbursts against the demon rum and his glorification of Prohibition diminished which naturally is linked to the negative consequences of Prohibition that caught Lovecraft by surprise. However, the fact that Prohibition did not have the desired effect was not the only influencing factor. A growing awareness of his personal idiosyncrasy and anachronism also had a part to play. By 1928 Lovecraft thought of himself as old fashioned, and his only point of contact with members of the younger generation was through an abstract philosophical or scientific lens. He was keenly aware that his tastes and habits were those of conservative country-gentry of centuries past and thus outmoded.[68]

Another influencing factor was as mentioned his growing interest in political philosophy and social reform. By 1934 it is evident from Lovecraft's correspondence that he sported an interest in 'reasonable economic change'. We also know that he renounced his arch-conservatism, saw himself as a

66 Ibid., 58.

67 It is important not to confuse socialism with communism in this respect. Lovecraft was certainly no communist and warned against it in his essays concerning political philosophy including 'Some Repetitions on the Times' dated 22 February 1933 and 'A Layman Looks at The Government' dated 22 November 1933. Both essays can be found in H. P. Lovecraft, *Collected Essays Volume 5: Philosophy, Autobiography & Miscellany*, S. T. Joshi, ed. (New York: Hippocampus Press, 2006), 85–111.

68 See Lovecraft's letter dated 13 February 1928 to Zealia Brown Reed Bishop in *The Spirit of Revision: Lovecraft's Letters to Zealia Brown Reed Bishop*, Sean Branney & Andrew Leman, eds (HPLHS, 2015), 104–105.

'rational socialist' and spoke in favour of supervised capitalism.[69] Likewise, he supported the rise of women in society and not only found the traditional subordination of women to be artificial but also that 'many qualities commonly regarded as innate – in races, classes, and sexes alike – are in reality results of habitual and imperceptible conditioning'.[70] In a letter to Robert H. Barlow dated 27 January 1937, he predicts a gradual and subtle change in society involving government guarantees of educational opportunities. According to Lovecraft such political reform will make money and antecedents less important and 'open a path toward achievement and position'.[71] The statement hints at a possible Romantic touch to Lovecraft's political deliberations because Rousseau who was one of the founding fathers of Romanticism and indeed also an Enlightenment thinker advocated the idea that the state should be able to interfere with the economy for the purpose of controlling rampant inequality and for preventing indulgence in luxury.[72] Furthermore, in *The Social Contract* Rousseau famously states that human beings may be unequal in strength and intelligence but become equal by covenant and right. This is followed by a passage claiming that with a bad government in charge equality is but an illusion that merely keeps the poor in their misery and sustains the rich in their usurpation.[73] This notion is somewhat echoed in Lovecraft's reflections on the downtrodden we saw earlier and his wish for a more equitable social order that could reduce the misery of the many.[74] Now it is important to understand

69 See H. P. Lovecraft's letter to Clark Ashton Smith dated 28 October 1934, in H. P. Lovecraft, *Selected Letters V 1934–1937*, August Derleth & James Turner, eds (Sauk City, WI: Arkham House Publishers, 1976), 57.

70 Ibid., 64.

71 See H. P. Lovecraft's letter to Robert H. Barlow dated 27 January 1937, in H. P. Lovecraft, *Selected Letters V 1934–1937*, August Derleth & James Turner, eds (Sauk City, WI: Arkham House Publishers, 1976), 388.

72 See Istvan Hont, *Politics in Commercial Society*, Béla Kapossy & Michael Sonenscher, eds (Cambridge, MA: Harvard University Press, 2015), 116, 118.

73 Jean-Jacques Rousseau, *The Social Contract* (London: Penguin Books, 1968), 68.

74 In this respect it is important to realise that equality is not purely a Romantic ideal and that it is not possible to categorise Lovecraft as a Romantic just because he is for a more equal society. Enlightenment thinkers such as John Locke and John Stuart Mill both advocated the notion. Locke in his opposition against the divine rights of kings and Mill argued that all human beings have equal need of a voice in society to

that *The Social Contract* is not a Romantic treatise but in fact a classical one and thus one cannot forge a link between Lovecraft and Romanticism based on the messages in *The Social Contract* alone. However, according to Berlin, what sets Rousseau apart from other Enlightenment thinkers and puts him in league with the Romantics is simply his manners and his temperament.[75] Lovecraft had a certain manner – a certain temperament and an intensity not unlike that of Rousseau. This is most detectable in his writings about teetotalism but also in a milder way in his later political musings. Consider the following:

> We must stop thinking primarily in terms of 'money' and 'business' – both artificial things– and begin to think increasingly in terms of actual resources and products on which 'money' and 'business' are based. In terms of these, of the human beings to whom they are to be distributed, and of the cognate human values which make the accidents of life and consciousness worth enduring.[76]

The last sentence I should think bears witness to Lovecraft's intensity as it suggests that Lovecraft is fully aware that life sometimes deals the individual unwanted cards, and that consciousness can be quite a burden.

Another example comes from the earlier mentioned 1934 letter to Clark Ashton Smith. Lovecraft writes:

> I have never believed that the securing of material resources ought to form the central interest of human life – but have instead maintained that *personality* is an independent flowering of the intellect and emotions wholly apart from the struggle of existence [...] My ideal in life is nothing material or quantitative, but simply the security and leisure necessary for the maximum flowering of the human spirit.[77]

---

secure their share of its benefits. See John Locke, *Two Treatises of Government*, Peter Laslett, ed. (Cambridge: Cambridge University Press, 1999), 269 and John Stuart Mill, *On Liberty* (London: Everyman, 1999), 314.

75 Berlin, *The Roots of Romanticism*, 52.

76 See H. P. Lovecraft, 'Some Repetitions on the Times', in *Collected Essays Volume 5: Philosophy, Autobiography & Miscellany*, S. T. Joshi, ed. (New York: Hippocampus Press, 2006), 86.

77 See H. P. Lovecraft's letter to Clark Ashton Smith dated 28 October 1934, in H. P. Lovecraft, *Selected Letters V 1934–1937*, August Derleth & James Turner, eds (Sauk City, WI: Arkham House Publishers, 1976), 60.

Here Lovecraft speaks intensely about his ideal in life which is not materialistic but wholeheartedly spiritual and very much Romantic. Lovecraft's focus is to flourish optimally and have the necessary security and free time to do so.

To wrap things up it seems fair to say that Lovecraft's teetotalism plays a significant part in his life story, philosophy and work. On a psychological level it is an indicator of what he feared the most, namely the beast within. He feared our animal appetites, and the idea that alcohol functions as a catalyst for bad behaviour kept him dry, fuelled his amateur journalism, propelled his poetry and use of 'hard likker' as a baneful trope in his fiction. On a political philosophical level, one might say that his crusade against alcohol in the long run served as a stimulus for change in his political attitude – a change that at least to my mind has a distinct Romantic air to it.

Bibliography

Aristotle, *The Nicomachean Ethics*, H. Rackham, trans., Loeb Classical Library (Cambridge, MA: Harvard University Press, 2003).

Berlin, Isaiah, *The Roots of Romanticism*, Henry Hardy, ed. (Princeton, NJ: Princeton University Press, 2001).

Cannon, Peter, ed., *Lovecraft Remembered* (Sauk City, WI: Arkham House Publishers, 1998).

The Charleston Observer, 10, no. 44 (29 October 1836), 174, Columns 4–5.

de Camp, L. Sprague, *Lovecraft: A Biography*, (New York: Doubleday, 1975).

Finn, Mark, *Blood and Thunder* (Austin: MonkeyBrain Books, 2006).

Gately, Iain, *Drink a Cultural History of Alcohol* (Sheridan, WY: Gotham Books, 2018).

Gough, John Bartholomew, *Sunlight and Shadow or Gleanings from My Life-Work* (London: Hodder and Stoughton, 1881).

The Holy Bible, King James Version (London: Tophi Books, 1994).

Horace, *Odes and Epodes*, Niall Rudd, trans., Loeb Classical Library (Cambridge, MA: Harvard University Press, 2004).

Joshi, S. T., *I Am Providence: The Life and Times of H. P. Lovecraft*, vol. 1 (New York: Hippocampus Press, 2010).

Joshi, S. T., ed., *Lovecraft Annual No. 5* (New York: Hippocampus Press, 2011).

Joshi, S. T., ed., *Lovecraft Annual No. 11* (New York: Hippocampus Press, 2017).

Joshi, S. T. & Schultz, David E., *An H. P. Lovecraft Encyclopedia* (New York: Hippocampus Press, 2001).

Locke, John, *Two Treatises of Government*, Peter Laslett, ed. (Cambridge: Cambridge University Press, 1999).

Lord, Evelyn, *The Hell-Fire Clubs: Sex, Satanism and Secret Societies* (New Haven, CT: Yale University Press, 2008).

Lovecraft, *H. P., Collected Essays Volume 1: Amateur Journalism*, S. T. Joshi, ed. (New York: Hippocampus Press, 2004).

Lovecraft, H. P., *Collected Essays Volume 5: Philosophy, Autobiography & Miscellany*, S. T. Joshi, ed. (New York: Hippocampus Press, 2006).

Lovecraft, H. P., 'Old Bugs', *The H. P. Lovecraft Archive*, <http://www.hplovecraft.com/writings/texts/fiction/ob.aspx>

Lovecraft, H. P., *Selected Letters I 1911–1924*, August Derleth & Donald Wandrei, eds (Sauk City, WI: Arkham House Publishers, 1965).

Lovecraft, H. P., *Selected Letters IV 1932–1934*, August Derleth & James Turner, eds (Sauk City, WI: Arkham House Publishers, 1976).

Lovecraft, H. P., *Selected Letters V 1934–1937*, August Derleth & James Turner, eds (Sauk City, WI: Arkham House Publishers, 1976).

Lovecraft, H. P., 'Sweet Ermengarde or the Heart of a Country Girl', *The H. P. Lovecraft Archive*, <http://www.hplovecraft.com/writings/texts/fiction/se.aspx>

Lovecraft, H. P., *The Ancient Track: The Complete Poetical Works of H. P. Lovecraft*, S. T. Joshi, ed. (New York: Hippocampus Press, 2013).

Lovecraft, H. P., *The New Annotated H. P. Lovecraft*, Leslie S. Klinger, ed. (New York: Liveright Publishing Corporation, 2014).

Lovecraft, H. P., *The New Annotated H. P. Lovecraft: Beyond Arkham*, Leslie S. Klinger, ed. (New York: Liveright Publishing Corporation, 2019).

Lovecraft, H. P. *The Spirit of Revision: Lovecraft's Letters to Zealia Brown Reed Bishop,* Sean Branney & Andrew Leman, eds (HPLHS, 2015).

MacCoun, Robert J. & Reuter, P., Drug War Heresies: Learning from Other Vices, Times, and Places (Cambridge: Cambridge University Press, 2001).

Mill, John Stuart, *On Liberty* (London: Everyman, 1999).

Nietzsche, Friedrich, Afgudernes ragnarok, Jens Erik Kristensen & Lars-Henrik Schmidt, trans. (Copenhagen: Gyldendal, 1999).

Nietzsche, Friedrich, *Beyond Good and Evil,* Walter Kaufmann, trans. (New York: Vintage Books, 1989).

Platon, *Platon I: Samlede værker i ny oversættelse*, Jørgen Mejer & Chr. Gorm Tortzen, eds (Copenhagen: Gyldendal, 2009).

Rorabaugh, W. J., *Prohibition: A Concise History* (Oxford: Oxford University Press, 2018).

Rousseau, Jean-Jacques, *The Social Contract* (London: Penguin Books, 1968).
Schmitt Carl, *Political Romanticism*, Guy Oakes, trans. (Cambridge, MA: MIT Press, 2011).
Seneca, *Moral Essays*, vol. II, John W. Basore, trans., Loeb Classical Library (Cambridge, MA: Harvard University Press, 1933).
Shakespeare, William, 'Othello', in *Tragedies*, vol. 1, Sylvan Barnet ed., (London: Everyman's Library, 1992).
Trotter, Thomas, *An Essay, Medical, Philosophical, and Chemical on Drunkenness and It's Effect on the Human Body* (London: Printed for T. N. Longman, and O. Rees, 1804).

CHAPTER 4

Lovecraft's Garden: Heart's Blood at the Root

Moving away from Lovecraft's teetotalism and political Romanticism, this chapter aims to bolster the notion that Lovecraft at heart was a Romantic via an entirely different route. The chapter begins with a preliminary sketch of the use of gardens in Romantic thought and the highlighting of six themes: contemplation, joy, the dramatic, the strange, the foreign and the beautiful that all underpin Romanticism.

This is followed by an elucidation of Lovecraft's fascination with gardens, his dealings in Romantic themes and what role they play in his short 1917 poem 'A Garden'.

The chapter concludes that given Lovecraft's love of gardens and that his poem 'A Garden' is imbued with Romantic themes and involves 'wondrous contemplation' and 'poetic knowledge', the case for his Romanticism has indeed been strengthened.

Romantic Gardens and Their Themes: A Primer

Gardens can be wonderful places and feature frequently in various kinds of literature including poetry and indeed philosophy, where they work as metaphors and function as in between places or vehicles of realisation and metamorphosis.

The famous twentieth-century American poet Robert Frost's short garden poem 'Lodged' addressing vulnerability and hardships is a prime example. The same goes for the stoic philosopher Seneca's somewhat passionate comments on the garden of Epicurus, which had a sign above its entrance reading: 'Stranger, here you will tarry; here our highest good is pleasure.'[1]

Gardens and indeed natural landscapes also play an important role in the Romantic Movement to the extent that we today operate with a type of garden labelled 'the Romantic garden'.

The Romantic garden contrasts with the symmetrical Baroque garden associated with sixteenth-century Italy and the seventeenth-century influential French aristocracy.[2] Unlike the Baroque garden where every aspect is controlled, manipulated and speaks of man's mastery over nature, the Romantic garden celebrates the unruliness of nature and enlarges the world of the person experiencing it. Thus, the Romantic garden symbolises a particular outlook and functions as a catalyst for Romantic philosophy. Contrasting the Baroque garden, the Romantic garden is not to be observed from above or from a distance, so that an adequate appraisal of its symmetry may be produced. It is to be wandered through and wondered at because it is a place that aims to reposition man within the realm of Pan, within nature and unlike the Baroque garden, it is a place of asymmetry, where one is reminded of the marvels of the world including things now distant and lost to us. Hence, Romantic gardens often include rare plants, ruins and temples of all sorts and kinds dedicated to ancient and 'forgotten' Gods.[3]

Not far from where I am writing these lines, one finds Søndermarken (The Southern Field) – a public park in Frederiksberg, Denmark. Established in the early eighteenth century, this is by many considered to

1 See Seneca, 'On the Renown Which My Writings Will Bring You', in *Epistles 1–65*, Richard M. Cummere, trans., Loeb Classical Library (Cambridge, MA: Harvard University Press, 1917), 147. Epicurus (341–270 BC) founded 'The Garden' which functioned both as school and a circle of friends. Epicurus is known for a rational hedonistic ethics urging one to strive towards pleasure in order to achieve well-being.

2 Villa Borghese gardens in Rome, Italy is a prime example of a Baroque garden and the same goes for the Gardens of Versailles in France.

3 See Nathalie de Harlez de Deulin, 'The Influence of England on the First English Gardens in the Southern Low Countries and the Principality of Liege', in *Garden History*, vol. 44, supplement 44 (Autumn 2016): Capability Brown: Perception and Response in Global Context: The Proceedings of an ICOMUS-UK Conference held at the University of Bath, 7–9 September 2016 (Autumn 2016), 96–97.

be the heart of Romanticism in Denmark because it was here the Danish poet and playwright Adam Oehlenschläger and his German friend; the philosopher, scientist and poet Henrich Steffens discussed new trends in German philosophy, including the thoughts of the German philosopher Friedrich Schelling. Schelling was one of the main driving forces in German Romanticism and had a profound influence on the English Romantic poet Samuel Taylor Coleridge. This becomes evident upon reading Coleridge's 1802 poem 'Dejection: An Ode' which is concerned with the loss of the shaping spirit of imagination and the joy that follows, by using this faculty.[4]

Furthermore, Coleridge, whom Lovecraft very much admired, is the author of the poem *The Rime of the Ancient Mariner* and he is important to Romantics as well as students of supernatural horror.[5] To the first because the (in)famous travelling Romantic Lord Byron identified himself with the ancient mariner.[6] To the latter because M. R. James, the English twentieth-century medievalist and ghost story writer, whom Lovecraft also admired, used it to great effect in his 1911 short story 'Casting the Runes'.[7]

Originally a Baroque garden, Søndermarken was changed into a Romantic garden in the years between 1780 and 1805 and back then, as today, it offers the visitor a glimpse into the Romantic fascination with themes including the dramatic, the strange, the foreign and the beautiful. There is, for example, a grotto, with a natural spring inside hinting at the Romantics fascination with ancient Greece and Rome and the promise of insight into mysteries that such animated places supposedly offered. One can also locate a memorial mound harbouring a statue of 'Mother Denmark' holding a baby. Surrounded by beautiful tall trees, it commemorates the Danes who long ago emigrated to America and chiselled above the

4 See Jan B. W. Pedersen, *Balanced Wonder: Experiential Sources of Imagination, Virtue, and Human Flourishing* (Lanham: Lexington Books 2019), 100–101.

5 Lovecraft, 'Supernatural Horror in Literature', 87.

6 See Carl Thomson, *The Suffering Traveller, and the Romantic Imagination* (Oxford: Clarendon Press, 2007), 60.

7 See H. P. Lovecraft, 'Supernatural Horror in Literature', in *Collected Essays/H. P. Lovecraft Volume 2: Literary Criticism*, S. T. Joshi, ed. (New York: Hippocampus Press, 2004), 123–124 & M. R. James, *Collected Ghost Stories*, Darryl Jones, ed. (Oxford: Oxford University Press, 2011), 160.

entrance of the mound one finds the dramatic inscription: 'They who set out, never to return.' Additionally, one may also find a strange Norwegian cabin, a Chinese pagoda and not forgetting the mysterious Cisterns – an early underground water reservoir now turned contemporary museum.

As an arboreal breathing space contrasting the artificiality of the surrounding city, Søndermarken serves as a refuge for the local fauna including different kinds of birds, rodents and insects, plus the frequent and all too human flaneur. All in all, Søndermarken is a precious and beneficial place as it caters to the contemplative mind and brings joy to many.

Now contemplation and joy are both complicated labels that deserve attention because both are beside the dramatic, the strange, the foreign and the beautiful: important Romantic themes.

Contemplation is difficult to understand and has been deliberated and celebrated since the Ancient peripatetic philosopher Aristotle taught at the Lyceum.[8] Furthermore, it has a close connection with the peculiar state of mind we call 'wonder' which was particularly important not only to the ancient Greek philosophers but also to the Romantics, and indeed Lovecraft.[9] To elaborate, let us take a brief look at philosopher Anders Schinkel's notion of 'contemplative wonder' which he understands as:

> A mode of consciousness in which we experience that which we perceive or are contemplating as strange, deeply other or mysterious, fundamentally beyond the limits of our understanding, yet worthy of attention for its own sake, in which our attention takes the form of an open receptive stance, and an attunement towards mystery.[10]

The term is insightful and praiseworthy because it makes clear that there could well be different kinds of wonderment. One might wonder how a combustion engine works, or what makes a helicopter fly, and such kinds of wonder correspond to what Schinkel labels 'inquisitive wonder'. Since both objects of wonder qualify as mechanical inventions one could in principle find out how they work.

8 The Lyceum was originally a sanctuary dedicated to Apollo but also a gymnasium. Book X of Aristotle's *Nicomachean Ethics* is concerned with contemplation.

9 See Chapters 1 and 2 and Pedersen, *Balanced Wonder*, 4, 32–34, 42.

10 Ander Schinkel, *Wonder and Education: On the Educational Importance of Contemplative Wonder* (London: Bloomsbury Academic, 2021), 54.

Another kind of wonder is as mentioned contemplative wonder, and this sort of wonderment Schinkel describes as:

> A 'silent' response to mystery, not immediately accompanied by an active search for answers; and at any rate there are no answers here, nothing that will dissolve the mystery or the wonder.[11]

The state of mind Schinkel is referring to could occur when pondering the concept of 'eternity' because can we truly understand what it is for something to be eternal? Some would point out what is eternal, is merely that which is not finite, but do we really know what it means to be finite or what it means for something to go out of existence? Naturally philosophical advancement or sophistication can be made, but ultimately it seems Schinkel is right that no matter what we do our action will not solve the mystery at hand.

Moving on, contemplative wonder is useful for our present purpose because if we flip it around and put 'wonder' before 'contemplation' we end up with another fusion, that is, 'wondrous contemplation'.

This is important because wondrous contemplation is the type of contemplation the Romantics and indeed Lovecraft advocated, experienced and sought. If we focus solely on the Romantic movement, one could say that wondrous contemplation served as the starting point of the movement because it is via such deep reflective introspective mental activity that Romanticism viewed as an attack on the enlightenment came about in the first place.[12] Furthermore, one could also hold that it is by means of contemplation that Romanticism as a rebellion against sixteenth-century philosopher Adam Smith's proclamation that human beings are labouring animals above and before all else arose.[13]

Now the critical reader could attempt a rebuke by interjecting that all this is merely superfluous sophistry or gratuitous conjunction and that

11 Ibid.

12 See Chapter 2 and Pedersen, *Balanced Wonder*, 4, 32.

13 See Berlin, *The Roots of Romanticism*,, 21 and Richard Adelman, *Idleness, Contemplation, and the Aesthetic, 1750–1830* (Cambridge: Cambridge University Press, 2011).

'wondrous contemplation', 'contemplative wonder', 'contemplation' and indeed 'wonder' merely refers to the same thing or mental phenomenon. I am sympathetic to such a stance, however, insofar there is such a thing as 'wondrous contemplation' it is important to realise that by distinguishing the term, we are engaged in the most praiseworthy art of taxonomy. A rock is never 'just' a rock because there are different kinds of rocks and so if we wish to advance our knowledge and understanding of rocks, we are forced to taxonomise and define igneous, sedimentary and so on. The same applies when we address mental activities such as wonder and contemplation because although they may look the same, they are not necessarily so. Having said that, the key to understand what wondrous contemplation is or what sets it aside from similar designations is introspection because as we shall see later in connection with Lovecraft's poem 'A Garden', wondrous contemplation leads to self-realisation and poetic knowledge.

Now joy is equally particular and important to the Romantics because as Coleridge claims; it is synonymous with the soul – it is the very power that animates us or gives us life as it transforms perception into feeling.[14] Paraphrasing the eminent philosopher Mary Warnock, one might say that without joy we only see, and regardless of whether we see an object as beautiful or not, we do so without feeling that it is one or the other.[15]

To exemplify imagine beholding the face of Leonardo da Vinci's most famous painting Mona Lisa. Realising that her face is beautiful is one thing but feeling that it is so, including that one can stare at her without grasping why she is so beautiful, is another. Naturally, the critic could put forth that the reason why one feels in such a way is purely because Leonardo cleverly incorporated the Fibonacci sequence in the painting. However, this does not take away the feeling at all. If anything, it encourages it because upon realising that the golden ratio plays a part in Mona Lisa's beauty we are left to wonder and contemplate the curious fact that since the sequence can be found in many a natural object including roses, ocean waves and spiral galaxies, Mona Lisa incorporates an aspect of the natural world that human beings are highly susceptible to and have an affinity for classifying

14 See Pedersen, *Balanced Wonder*, 101.

15 Mary Warnock, *Imagination* (London: Faber & Faber, 1976), 78.

as beautiful. In this light one must now consider if there is an objective ring to the notion of beauty and by extension, ugliness, that goes beyond mere matters of taste.

Considering the above we are now at liberty to say that the Romantic traveller who saunters around in places such as Søndermarken, observing the sights, in doing so becomes an honourable figure because his or her very activity, including the search for the dramatic, the strange, the foreign and the beautiful is closely connected to the complex workings of contemplation and joy.

Lovecraft's Romantic Bent: An Advance

The gentleman of Providence was no stranger to the above-mentioned Romantic themes including contemplation, and the search for joy which fuelled many valuable adventures to places outside his beloved Providence including Cape Cod, Charleston, Key West, Marblehead, New Orleans, Quebec, Salem and Vermont.[16]

Despite his reputation as a recluse, Lovecraft was quite outgoing and held the woodlands of New England in October in high esteem. Likewise,

16 See S. T. Joshi's, 'Introduction' and Lovecraft's essay 'Charleston', in H. P. Lovecraft *Collected Essays Volume 4: Travel*, S. T. Joshi, ed. (New York: Hippocampus Pres, 2005), 7, 261. See also Lovecraft's letter to Reinhardt Kleiner dated 11 January 1923, in Lovecraft, *Selected Letters I 1911–1924*, 203–206 and his letter to Wilfred Blanch Talman dated 10 December 1930, in H. P. Lovecraft, *Selected Letters III 1929–1931*, August Derleth & Donald Wandrei (Sauk City, WI: Arkham House Publishers, 1971), 239. Naturally not all such adventures were successful and one noteworthy and exhausting misadventure is the mysterious 1923 trip to 'Dark Swamp', a blighted somewhat wild area close to Chepachet, Rhode Island. For more information see C. M. Eddy, Jr, 'Walks with H. P. Lovecraft', in *Lovecraft Remembered*, Peter Cannon, ed. (Sauk City, WI: Arkham House Publishers, 1998), 67–68; Lovecraft's letter to Frank Belknap Long in Lovecraft, *Selected Letters I 1911–1924*, 149 and Stephen Olbrys Gencarella's, 'Lovecraft and the Folklore of Glocester's Dark Swamp', in *Lovecraft Annual No. 16*, S. T. Joshi, ed. (New York: Hippocampus Pres, 2022). 90–127.

he had an affinity for Wade Park in Cleveland, and the Japanese garden located in Brooklyn.[17] In 1930 he found his ideal garden at Maymont – a Victorian estate in Richmond, Virginia and in a most joyous and enthusiastic letter to Alfred Galpin dated 15 May the same year he writes:

> Gad, Sir, I swoon! I swoon with the conscious contemplation of complete and culminant beauty [...] This is something to see and dream about all the rest of one's life. I am sure I shall think of very little else during my few remaining days! It is Poe's *Domain of Arnheim* and *Island of the Fay* all roll into one –with my own Cathuria and gardens of Yin added for good measure.[18]

Besides revealing his love for Poe's work and flashing elements of his own creations including the wondrous 'Cathuria' – the land of hope from the short dreamland story 'The White Ship' (1919) and 'The garden of Yin' – sonnet number 18 from his curious collection of poetry entitled 'Fungi from Yuggoth', the letter discloses Lovecraft's appreciation of gardens and attention to contemplation and joy. Additionally, his enthusiastic confessions concerning the beauty of Maymont, reveal his Romanticism and rich, emotional life. Lovecraft held the experience of walking through gardens as one of the supreme incarnations of what he calls 'utter perfect beauty', and this singular deep-felt focus on the notion of beauty ties him to the Romantics to whom beauty was to be treasured.[19] In the same letter to Galpin he elaborates:

17 See H. P. Lovecraft October 1928 letter August Derleth in *Selected Letters II 1925–1929*, August Derleth & Donald Wandrei, eds (Sauk City, WI: Arkham House Publishers, 1968), 248 and his letter to Alfred Galpin dated 15 May 1930, in Lovecraft, *Selected Letters III 1929–1931*, 149.

18 See H. P. Lovecraft's letter to Alfred Galpin dated 15 May 1930, in Lovecraft, *Selected Letters III 1929–1931*, 149. Lovecraft's enthusiasm in relation to Maymont was so intense that he more or less repeated his wording in a letter sent to James Ferdinand Morton on the same day. See Lovecraft, *Selected Letters III 1929–1931*, 150.

19 Ibid. Lord Byron's lyrical and most celebrated poem 'She Walks in Beauty' is a testimony of the importance of beauty in Romantic thought. The same goes for German Romantic philosopher par excellence Immanuel Kant's distinction between beauty and the sublime penned in his *The Critique of Judgement*. In §23 he notes that beauty relates to the form of the object. The sublime is different in the sense that it is represented by boundlessness—something we cannot quantify like

> The experience of walking (or, as in most of my dreams, aerially floating) through aethereal and enchanted gardens of exotic delicacy and opulence, with carved stone, bridges, labyrinthine paths, marble fountains, terraces and staircases, strange pagodas, hillside grottos, curious statues, termini, sundials, benches, basins and lanthorns, lily'd pools of swans and streams with tiers of waterfalls, spreading gingko-trees and dropping, feathery willows, and sun-touch'd flowers of bizarre, Klarkash-Tonick pattern never beheld on land or beneath the sea ....[20]

The Romantic notion of walking though gardens engaging in contemplation and the enjoyment of beauty was clearly important to Lovecraft and a returning leitmotif in his literary work.

Consider his early prose poem 'Ex Oblivione' (1921) which he wrote under the pseudonym of Ward Phillips. In the story, the narrator finds in the dreamlands some of the beauty he vainly sought in life, as he wanders through old gardens and enchanted woods.[21]

Lovecraft's last story 'The Haunter of the Dark (1936), features the protagonist Robert Blake that upon returning to Providence takes up the upper floor of a respected house in a grassy court of College Street. Lovecraft describes it as 'a cosy and fascinating place, in a little garden oasis of village-like antiquity where huge, friendly cats sunned themselves atop a convenient shed'.[22] Later on in the spring when Blake has begun his long-planned novel, he finds himself strangely unable to make progress. He would sit at his westward window and 'when the delicate leaves came out on the garden boughs the world was filled with a new beauty'.[23] Of course, one might say that there is not much going on in terms of wandering through beautiful gardens in 'The Haunter of the Dark', but the point is that the notion of being situated in a beautiful life-giving place was something

the misty surroundings of the lonely wanderer in Caspar Friedrich's famous 1818 painting *Der Wanderer über dem Nebelmeer.*

20 Ibid., 149.

21 See H. P. Lovecraft's, 'Ex Oblivione', in *The New Annotated H. P. Lovecraft: Beyond Arkham*, Leslie S. Klinger, ed. (New York: Liveright Publishing Corporation, 2019), 86.

22 See H. P. Lovecraft, 'The Haunter of the Dark', in *The New Annotated H. P. Lovecraft*, Leslie S. Klinger, ed. (New York: Liveright Publishing Corporation, 2014), 781.

23 Ibid., 784.

Lovecraft contemplated and found important as much in 1935, two years before his passing, as it was in 1921 when he wrote 'Ex Oblivione'. In this light Lovecraft comes across as an enduring Romantic, which is important to our understanding of him as a person.[24]

Romantic Qualities in Lovecraft's Short Stories and Poetry: A Precis

Several of Lovecraft's stories have a Romantic ring to them, because they are centred on contemplative characters searching for joy.

One such story is 'The Strange High House in the Mist' (1931) which focuses on the restless philosopher Thomas Olney who taught ponderous

24 We find some of the same thoughts and feelings in 1921 short story 'The Moon Bog' where Lovecraft reveals the details of a wonderful dream experienced by the narrator centred around a stately city in a green valley where, 'marble streets and statues, villas and temples, carvings and inscriptions, all spoke in certain tones the glory that was Greece'. See H. P. Lovecraft, 'The Moon Bog', in *Eldritch Tales: A Miscellany of the Macabre*, Stephen Jones, ed. (London: Gollancz, 2011), 199. Greece or the idea that is Greece is a pivotal point for the great poets of the Romantic movement as well as for Lovecraft. Lord Byron's narrative poem 'Childe Harold's Pilgrimage' published in the beginning of the nineteenth century reveals the melancholic thoughts and feelings of a disillusioned traveller and points out the grandeur of Greece. See Lord Byron, 'Childe Harold's Pilgrimage', in *The Complete Poetical Works*, vol. III, Jerome J. McGann, ed. (Oxford: Clarendon Press, 1980), canto II. John Keats likewise celebrated Greece in his 1819 poem 'Ode on a Grecian Urn' which influence both Lovecraft and Anna Helen Crofts who incorporated its ending: 'beauty is truth, truth beauty,—that is all Ye know on earth, and all ye need to know' into their 1920 short story 'Poetry of the Gods'. See John Keats, *The Complete Poetry and Selected Prose of John Keats*, Harold E. Briggs, ed. (New York: Random House, 1951), V. 50 and H. P. Lovecraft with Anna Helen Crofts, 'Poetry and the Gods', in *Eldritch Tales: A Miscellany of the Macabre*, Stephen Jones, ed. (London: Gollancz, 2011), 88.

things in a college by Narragansett Bay, and one summer found unexpected joy in the ancient house mentioned in the title of the story.[25]

Another story is 'The Quest of Iranon' (1935) that tracks the exploits of Iranon – the travelling protagonist, who questions the ways of the god(s) fearing hardworking men of Teloth. Iranon asks:

> Wherefore do ye toil; is it not that ye may live and be happy? And if ye toil only that ye may toil more, when shall happiness find you? Ye toil to live, but is not life made of beauty and song? And if ye suffer no singers among you, where shall be the fruits of your toil? Toil without song is like a weary journey without an end. Were not death more pleasing?[26]

Both Olney and Iranon are thoughtful seekers that question the ways of people around them, and through both we become acquainted with some of Lovecraft's innermost Romantic sentiments and longings.

As mouthpieces of Lovecraft both characters are in a sense philosopher kings or Romantics par excellence although they enjoy/suffer radically different fates. Both have fathomed the 'enslaving' machinery we call culture and have in a sense broken free. However, where Olney finds the contentment and joy, he seeks, Iranon ultimately fails in doing so, and ceases to exist following a moment of devastating self-understanding.[27] This does not

25 See H. P. Lovecraft, 'The Strange High House in the Mist', in *The New Annotated H. P. Lovecraft: Beyond Arkham*, Leslie S. Klinger, ed. (New York: Liveright Publishing Corporation, 2019), 301–310.

26 See H. P. Lovecraft, 'The Quest of Iranon', in *The New Annotated H. P. Lovecraft: Beyond Arkham*, Leslie S. Klinger, ed. (New York: Liveright Publishing Corporation, 2019), 191.

27 Ibid., 96. The fate of Olney is mysterious as he in a sense gets split in two. 'Olney 1' stays at the strange high house in the mist and indulges in joys beyond earth's joys. See H. P. Lovecraft, 'The Strange High House in the Mist', in *The New Annotated H. P. Lovecraft: Beyond Arkham*, Leslie S. Klinger, ed. (New York: Liveright Publishing Corporation, 2019), 308. 'Olney 2' who walks into Kingsport the next day is something else entirely because he is utterly complacent, and one wonders if this phantom doubleganger indeed is the real Olney. This question becomes more pressing as the story moves forward because we learn that 'Olney 2' simply became whatever society and his family wanted him to be; that he no longer sought secrets or the magic of farther hills. Furthermore, Lovecraft reveals that 'Olney 2' bore the sameness of his days without complaints and that his well-disciplined thoughts

make him less of a Romantic, because discomfort, suffering and failure are fully fledged Romantic trappings as they make for a tragic hero.[28]

Let us now turn attention to an even earlier poem by Lovecraft, 'A Garden' (1917), while keeping in mind the above-mentioned Romantic themes. The poem read as follows.

> There's an ancient, ancient garden that I see sometimes in dreams,
> Where the very Maytime sunlight plays and glows with spectral gleams;
> Where the gaudy-tinted blossoms seem to wither into grey,
> And the crumbling walls and pillars waken thoughts of yesterday.
> There are vines in nooks and crannies, and there's moss about the pool,
> And the tangled weedy thicket chokes the arbour dark and cool:
> In the silent sunken pathways springs an herbage sparse and spare,
> While the musty scent of dead things dulls the fragrance of the air.
> There is not a living creature in the lonely space around,
> And the hedge-encompass'd quiet never echoes to a sound.
> As I walk, and wait, and listen, I will often seek to find
> When it was I knew that garden in an age long left behind;
> I will oft conjure a vision of a day that is no more,
> As I gaze upon the grey, grey scenes I feel I knew before.
> Then a sadness settles o'er me, and a tremor seems to start:
> For I know the flow'rs are shrivell'd hopes – the garden is my heart![29]

---

which bored him so, before he ascended the crag and came face to face with the entity dwelling in the strange high house in the mist became enough for him. At the end of the story, we likewise learn that 'Olney 2' eventually together with his family moves to a bungalow at Bristol Highlands where everything is urban and modern and is never heard of again. Ibid., 308–309. This is an important detail, and the keyword here is 'modern' because already in 1919 Lovecraft thought himself an antique personality and not a modern one. See H. P. Lovecraft's letter to Reinhardt Kleiner dated 12 August 1919, in Lovecraft, *Selected Letters I 1911–1924*, 84–85. Thus, via the fate of Olney, we get a glimpse into Lovecraft's Romanticism—his longing for something more. In their work on 'The Strange High House in the Mist' Lovecraft scholars S. T. Joshi and David E. Schultz pinpoints that Olney realises while in the house that he belongs in realm of 'nebulous wonder'. I think that this corresponds to Lovecraft himself as well. See Joshi & Schultz, *An H. P. Lovecraft Encyclopedia*, 253.

28 See Thomson, *The Suffering Traveller, and the Romantic Imagination*, 58.

29 H. P. Lovecraft, 'A Garden', in *The Ancient Track: The Complete Poetical Works of H. P. Lovecraft*, S. T. Joshi, ed. (New York: Hippocampus Pres, 2013), 278.

The poem stands as evidence of Lovecraft's Romanticism because it deals in all the Romantic themes mentioned thus far and, in the following, I shall elaborate on each theme in turn, saving contemplation and joy for last.

Now the poem is dramatic, primarily because of the lamentation and loss it conveys. Furthermore, it stages a gloomy and most dramatic atmosphere much like the beginning of Edgar Allan Poe's gothic tale *The Fall of the House of Usher* where the protagonist during a dull, dark and soundless autumn day passes alone through a dreary track of the country only to end up at the melancholy House of Usher.[30]

This dramatic poem also shares a confessional tone with the opening stanza of Wordsworth's Romantic poem 'Ode: Intimations of Immortality' which reads:

> There was a time when meadow, grove, and stream,
> The earth, and every common sight,
>   To me did seem
>   Apparelled in celestial light,
> The glory and the freshness of a dream.
> It is not now as it has been of yore; –
>   Turn wheresoe'er I may,
>   By night or day,
> The things which I have seen I now can see no more.[31]

Lovecraft's 'A Garden' and Wordsworth's 'Ode: Intimations of Immortality' both express the same mood; the same intense notion of a paradise lost or the drama surrounding the pain of lost things.

Now Wordsworth's poem, given the framework of this chapter is much too lengthy for adequate treatment, but it ends, after a rollercoaster

30 Edgar Allan Poe, 'The Fall of the House of Usher', in *The Portable Poe*, Philip van Doren Stern, ed. (New York: Penguin Books, 1977), 244.

31 See William Wordsworth, 'Ode: Intimations of Immortality', in *The Major Works* (Oxford: Oxford University Press, 2011), 297.

ride filled with melancholic realisations and enthusiastic appreciations, on a positive and wise note.

Lovecraft's 'A Garden' is dramatic, but very different. It is short in comparison and resembles in its message merely the first stanza of 'Ode: Intimations of Immortality' which thoroughly communicates the gloomy disposition of the poetic confessor.

Lovecraft's poem also differs from Wordsworth's in the sense that where Wordsworth's melancholy and gradual change of perspective seems conceived amidst beautiful scenery, Lovecraft's poem comes across as a perplexing introspective ramble through a desolate dream country culminating in an upsetting moment of stark self-realisation where it is revealed that the garden metaphorically speaking is in fact Lovecraft's own heart.[32]

Adding to the drama, one can say that the last line represents a truly remarkable moment in Lovecraft's authorship, because it shows a Lovecraft far removed from the supposedly 'supremely unemotional' character that he later claims to be – a character that does 'not weep or indulge in lugubrious demonstrations of the vulgar'.[33] The closing line unveils a tenderness and a Romantic quality to Lovecraft that is generally unsung. It speaks of the inner dramatic workings of Lovecraft's mind and the intense feelings he harboured, and a longing for something that once was or had never been.

32 Lovecraft also put the mechanism to use in the short story 'The Outsider' (1926) where the narrator after much wandering through bleak and austere environments at the end face a most unwelcome truth in the form of a mirror and the realisation that he is indeed a monster. See H. P. Lovecraft, 'The Outsider', in *The New Annotated H. P. Lovecraft: Beyond Arkham*, Leslie S. Klinger, ed. (New York: Liveright Publishing Corporation, 2019), 104.

33 See H. P. Lovecraft's letter to Mrs Anne Tillery Renshaw dated 1 June 1921, in Lovecraft, *Selected Letters I 1911–1924*, 133.

Figure 4.1 Harry Evans, *Caisleán*, 2023. Courtesy of Harry Evans.

Lovecraft's poem 'A Garden' is Romantic because it deals in the strange and the foreign and there are three reasons for this. First, the garden is strange and foreign because it is idiosyncratic to Lovecraft in the sense that it is not a garden the reader can readily visit and form an opinion about independently of Lovecraft's description. Thus 'A Garden' is not a clear-cut case of topographical poetry like John Dyers's 1726 poem 'Grongar Hill', but a piece of poetry twice removed from our common experiential world in the sense that it takes the reader on a voyage into both Lovecraft's dreamworld and lifeworld as only he conceives and experiences it. In turn this promotes alienation – have us think of the poem as strange and foreign at least until the closing line where the author and reader come together in a fellowship of understanding about the fragility of the heart.

Secondly, the lines 'There is not a living creature in the lonely space around, And the hedge-encompassed'd quiet never echoes to a sound' speak of a place strange and foreign to us. Most people live out their lives in environments rich in life and sound. Human beings are social creatures and thus we are drawn to lively places such as bars, cafes, clubs, markets and public houses because here we meet with others of our kind which is important for our flourishing as human beings.

Thirdly the line describing the crumbling walls and pillars that wakens thoughts of yesterday deals in the strange and the foreign because what Lovecraft is talking about is ruins. As mentioned earlier, ruins and the appreciation of such is an established theme within Romanticism, because ruins speak of bygone things and cater to the contemplative, reflective and `wundersüchtig' mind (see Figure 4.1).[34] Lovecraft uses the ruins to help us connect to the notion of the distant past and to build an atmosphere of strangeness and alienation which in turn drives the poem towards its painful and surprising conclusion.

Upon realising that the garden represents Lovecraft's very own heart, the ruins take on a strange new dimension and have us think of them not as remnants from the past external to Lovecraft, but as representations of Lovecraft's personal ruin and tragedy which, qua their idiosyncrasy, comes across as truly foreign indeed.

Because Lovecraft's 'A Garden' incorporates the notion of beauty it can also be classified as Romantic, but Romantic beauty is something special as it is interwoven with ugliness. In this regard it is important to understand that Romanticism is littered with dichotomies meaning that the Romantic vision tends to pendulate between two poles that not only inform the other but also convey a unique philosophy or vision aiming at resolving antithesis.[35] This is the reason why Romantic works often contain contrasts or direct opposites such as life and death, heart and reason, misery and happiness, and indeed beauty and ugliness.

To illustrate, consider Charles-Auguste Mengin's 1867 painting *Sappho* which depicts the radiant beauty of the ancient Greek poet Sappho against an ugly threatening background (see Figure 4.2). What makes the painting

34 In his biography L. Sprague, de Camp is using this German word term to describe Lovecraft and it roughly refers to someone who has an affinity for the supernatural or that which lies just beyond our senses. See L. Sprague de Camp, *Lovecraft: A Biography* (New York: Doubleday, 1975), 20.

35 See Umberto Eco, *On Beauty: A History of a Western Idea* (London: Secker & Warburg, 2004), 299.

alluring and Romantic is partly that the threatening background highlights Sappho's beauty which in turn lends an extra offensive dimension to the background. To illustrate this further suppose we were to change the background and set Sappho against a lush and peaceful backdrop then one could rightly wonder if her beauty would not somehow change in quality – perhaps even fade a little.

The same can be said of the gloomy background. Imagine if Sappho was depicted with a hideous face like the plague in Arnold Böcklin's 1898 eponymous painting or after a fashion resembling the uncanny white malformed ape or anthropomorphic fiend from Lovecraft's 'Reanimator'. Would it not change the aesthetic quality of the background? Would it not diminish some of the ugliness, leaving us with an entirely different experience or aesthetic judgement?

Why bring all this up? Well, Lovecraft's 'A Garden' plays with beauty and ugliness the same way Mengin's *Sappho* does.[36] In 'A Garden' ugliness is used first to make us aware of the quality the garden lacks, that is, beauty. This takes up most of the poem and is quite overwhelming as we are guided from one ugliness to another and hear about everything from how the Maytime sunlight glows with spectral gleams to how the musty scent of dead things dulls the fragrance of the air and how the narrator often conjures up a vision of a day that is no more.

Secondly, the focus on ugliness in the poem serves the purpose of strengthening the impact and beauty of the closing line where we learn that the ruined garden corresponds to Lovecraft's heart. As a whole 'A Garden' conjures up an awareness akin to Mengin's *Sappho* in the sense that as

36 In his lifework Lovecraft often dealt with beauty and ugliness separately and earlier we saw how he used the word 'beauty' in connection with his report to Alfred Galpin concerning the garden in Maymont. He also focused on beauty in 'Ex Oblivione' where the narrator found some of the beauty he vainly sought in life in the mysterious dreamlands. In terms of Lovecraft's dealings in ugliness the predicate appears in his campaign against alcohol where he simply labels drink 'ugly'. See Chapter 3. Likewise, he uses the word 'ugly' in his signature piece of fiction 'The Call of Cthulhu' to describe the roots and malignant hanging nooses of Spanish moss the police faced during their search for the Louisiana swamp worshippers. See 'The Call of Cthulhu', in *The New Annotated H. P. Lovecraft*, Leslie S. Klinger, ed. (New York: Liveright Publishing Corporation, 2014), 138.

much as we can acknowledge that Sappho's beauty is enhanced by the ugly background, we can acknowledge that the beauty of the last sentence in 'A Garden' is enhanced by the overwhelming ugliness described beforehand.

One might even say that the ugliness of the garden contrasting the beauty of the last sentence helps us recognise that Lovecraft the poet harbours a most sensitive and beautiful mind despite his melancholy. It helps us to see that the gentleman of Providence is indeed a Romantic.

Figure 4.2. Charles Auguste Mengin, *Sappho*, 1877.

'A Garden' likewise portrays Lovecraft as a Romantic because it deals in contemplation and joy.

That the poem is contemplative in nature is clear for at least two reasons. The first and most obvious one is linked to the passage reading: 'As I walk, and wait, and listen, I will often seek to find when it was I knew that garden in an age long left behind.' The narrator is perplexed by the uncanny, yet strangely familiar location and he is trying his best to find out where he is by observing the surrounding dreamscape which inspires nothing but a strange sense of familiarity.

The second reason is due to its powerful closing line, because this line induces a focus-shift from the curious dreamscape to the narrator himself, whose unknown past and plans for life suddenly become of immense importance to the reader and key to understanding what or who the poem is all about.

At first it may seem an overstatement of cyclopean proportion to categorise the poem as joyful because how can ugliness and desolation even remotely communicate joy? The answer is twofold and connected to the remarkable closing line, the state of mind we call 'wonder' and indeed 'wondrous contemplation'.

The poem is joyful because of the utter surprise of the closing line. This does not mean that we must draw enjoyment from Lovecraft's broken heart, nor am I referring to schadenfreude. What makes the line joyful is the fact that it is an anomaly to hear Lovecraft speak of his heart in such a manner, and consequently it makes the heart of the reader leap up in the same fashion as Wordsworth's did when he beheld a rainbow in the sky.[37] Like the rainbow, it is a wonder to behold Lovecraft speak in this manner and it inflicts a crack in our conception of Lovecraft, leaving the gentleman of Providence mysterious and undefined. The closing line has us realise that our knowledge of him is broken – that our understanding of him is incomplete and that instigates wonder, which in turn evokes joy.[38]

Additionally, one can argue that the closing line is joyful because it is a testimony of Lovecraft's wondrous contemplation in action. Unlike Schinkel's 'contemplative wonder' that does not produce anything new, 'wondrous contemplation' indeed does produce something new in terms of self-realisation and poetic knowledge which literary scholar James S. Taylor defines as:

37 See William Wordsworth, 'My Heart Leaps Up When I Behold', in *The Major Works* (Oxford: Oxford University Press, 2008), 246.

38 For more information on the relationship between wonder and joy see Pedersen, *Balanced Wonder*, 1–10.

> A spontaneous act of external and internal senses with the intellect, integrated and whole, rather than an act associated with the power of analytic reasoning.[39]

Since the bleak garden is a returning dream, and given that the narrator is Lovecraft himself, the realisation at the end of the poem is the result of Lovecraft's observations and analysis of the dreamscape in conjunction with introspection, an active search though his own memory palace. The purpose of this sophisticated engagement is simply to grasp what the garden is and the terrific reveal or self-realisation at the end of the poem is, although seemingly surprising to Lovecraft, not exclusively a horrifying one. Indeed, it is also wonderful and even therapeutic because it moves Lovecraft forward, in the sense that he now understands an important point about himself and his life. In this sense the ending of the poem converges into a moment of truth – a moment of poetic knowledge where what is good, what is beautiful, and what is true, all come together. This is a truly wonderful point in Lovecraft's work – a joyful high point signifying the importance of Professor Parkins from M. R. James' short story 'Oh, Whistle, and I'll Come to You, My Lad' learned statement extrapolating that truth is never offensive.[40]

Summary: A Closure

Gardens play a significant role in Romanticism and Lovecraft's love of gardens together with his dealings in the dramatic, the strange, the foreign, the beautiful, as well as contemplation and joy all underpins his Romanticism. Boldly stated all the above culminates in his short poem 'A Garden' – a poem imbued with Romantic themes that until now has been somewhat unnoticed by Lovecraft scholars.

39 See James S. Taylor, *Poetic Knowledge: The Recovery of Education* (New York: State University of New York Press, 1998), 6.

40 See M. R. James, 'Oh, Whistle, and I'll Come to You, My Lad', in *Collected Ghost Stories*, Darryl Jones, ed. (Oxford: Oxford University Press, 2011), 76.

Earlier I argued that Lovecraft was a Romantic 'on the Nightside' given his enormous contribution to weird fiction. With this chapter now coming to a close, it is evident that the view of Lovecraft as a Romantic has been strengthened especially when we consider his dealings in wondrous contemplation and poetic knowledge. To end I should think it fitting to echo Keats and say that wondrous contemplation is poetic knowledge, poetic knowledge wondrous contemplation – that is all Ye know on earth, and all ye need to know.

Bibliography

Adelman, Richard, *Idleness, Contemplation, and the Aesthetic, 1750–1830* (Cambridge: Cambridge University Press, 2011).

Berlin, Isaiah, *The Roots of Romanticism*, Henry Hardy, ed. (Princeton, NJ: Princeton University Press, 2001).

Byron, Lord, *The Complete Poetical Works*, vol III, Jerome J. McGann, ed. (Oxford: Clarendon Press, 1980).

Cannon, Peter, ed., *Lovecraft Remembered* (Sauk City, WI: Arkham House Publishers, 1998).

De Camp, Sprague L., *Lovecraft: A Biography* (New York: Doubleday, 1975).

De Deulin, Nathalie de Harlez, 'The Influence of England on the First English Gardens in the Southern Low Countries and the Principality of Liege', in *Garden History*, vol. 44, supplement 44 (Autumn 2016): *Capability Brown: Perception and Response in Global Context: The Proceedings of an ICOMUS-UK Conference held at the University of Bath*, 7–9 September 2016 (Autumn 2016).

Eco, Umberto, *On Beauty: A History of a Western Idea* (London: Secker & Warburg, 2004).

James, M. R. *Collected Ghost Stories*, Darryl Jones, ed. (Oxford: Oxford University Press, 2011).

Joshi, S. T., ed., *Lovecraft Annual No. 16* (New York: Hippocampus Press, 2022).

Joshi, S. T. & Schultz, David E., *An H. P. Lovecraft Encyclopedia* (New York: Hippocampus Press, 2001).

Kant, Immanuel, *Critique of Judgement*, W. S. Pluhar, trans. (Cambridge: Hackett Publishing, 1987).

Keats, John, *The Complete Poetry and Selected Prose of John Keats*, Harold E. Briggs, ed. (New York: Random House, 1951).
Lovecraft, H. P., *Collected Essays Volume 2: Literary Criticism*, S. T. Joshi, ed. (New York: Hippocampus Press, 2004).
Lovecraft, H. P., *Collected Essays Volume 4: Travel*, S. T. Joshi, ed. (New York: Hippocampus Press, 2005).
Lovecraft, H. P., *Eldritch Tales: A Miscellany of the Macabre*, Stephen Jones, ed. (London: Gollancz, 2011).
Lovecraft, H. P., *Selected Letters I 1911–1924*, August Derleth & Donald Wandrei, eds (Sauk City, WI: Arkham House Publishers, 1965).
Lovecraft, H. P., *Selected Letters II 1925–1929*, August Derleth & Donald Wandrei, eds (Sauk City, WI: Arkham House Publishers, 1968).
Lovecraft, H. P. *Selected Letters III 1929–1931*, August Derleth & Donald Wandrei, eds (Sauk City, WI: Arkham House Publishers, 1971).
Lovecraft, H. P., *The Ancient Track: The Complete Poetical Works of H. P. Lovecraft*, S. T. Joshi, ed. (New York: Hippocampus Press, 2013).
Lovecraft, H. P., *The New Annotated H. P. Lovecraft*, Leslie S. Klinger, ed. (New York: Liveright Publishing Corporation, 2014).
Lovecraft, H. P., *The New Annotated H. P. Lovecraft: Beyond Arkham*, Leslie S. Klinger, ed. (New York: Liveright Publishing Corporation, 2019).
Pedersen, Jan B. W., *Balanced Wonder: Experiential Sources of Imagination, Virtue, and Human Flourishing* (Lanham: Lexington Books, 2019).
Poe, Edgar Allan, *The Portable Poe*, Philip van Doren Stern, ed. (New York: Penguin Books, 1977).
Seneca, *Epistles 1–65*, Richard M. Cummere, trans., Loeb Classical Library (Cambridge, MA: Harvard University Press, 1917).
Schinkel, Anders, *Wonder and Education: On the Educational Importance of Contemplative Wonder* (London: Bloomsbury Academic, 2021).
Taylor, James S., *Poetic Knowledge: The Recovery of Education* (New York: State University of New York Press, 1998).
Thomson, Carl, *The Suffering Traveller, and the Romantic Imagination* (Oxford: Clarendon Press, 2007).
Warnock, Mary, *Imagination* (London: Faber & Faber, 1976).
Wordsworth, William, *The Major Works* (Oxford: Oxford University Press, 2011).

CHAPTER 5

Weird Fiction: A Catalyst for Wonder

One of the vexing questions in the philosophy of wonder and indeed education is how to ensure that the next generation harbours a sense of wonder. Wonder is important, we think, because it encourages inquiry and keeps us as Albert Einstein would argue from 'being as good as dead' or 'snuffed-out candles'.[1] But how is an educator to install, bring to life, or otherwise encourage a sense of wonder in his or her students? Biologist Rachel Carson suggests that exploring nature and specifically undertaking walks along the rocky coast of Maine would keep alive a person's inborn sense of wonder.[2] Philosopher Jesse Prinz thinks that exposure to art will encourage wonderment because artworks, as he puts it, are 'inventions for feeding the appetite that wonder excites in us'.[3] Weird fiction (a subgenre of speculative fiction) – and in particular the work of one of its greatest exponents, the early twentieth-century American author Howard Phillips Lovecraft – is likewise a catalyst for wonder. The reason behind this is that Lovecraft's 'wonder-stories' are densely packed with wonder per design; in support of this claim, I shall in what is to come begin by elaborating on Lovecraft's 'wonder-full' weird fiction. Secondly, I shall clarify what is meant by something being 'densely packed with wonder' via bringing to the fore evidence of Lovecraft's literary wondermongery. Thirdly I will reflect on the notion of 'dark wonder' and Dark Romanticism and offer reasons why 'dark wonder' is suitable for the kind of wonder we find in Lovecraft's work. Finally, I shall clarify why exposure

1 Albert Einstein, *The World as I See It* (New York: The Wisdom Library, 1949), 5.

2 Rachel Carson, *The Sense of Wonder* (New York: HarperCollins, 1984).

3 Jesse Prinz, 'How Wonder Works', *Aeon Magazine* (2013), <http://aeon.co/magazine/psychology/why-wonder-is-the-most-human-of-all-emotions/>, accessed 2 July 2019.

to wonder and even wonder of the darker kind can be edifying, and in that sense educational.

Lovecraft and Weird Fiction

Lovecraft published his fiction more or less exclusively in American pulp magazines of the 1920s and 1930s including *Astounding Stories*, *Weird Tales* and *Wonder Stories*, and as mentioned in the first chapter his writing is roughly speaking designed to evoke either terror, horror, or wonder in the reader. Terror, horror and wonder are extraordinary states of mind because they are not states we experience all the time. They are rare and distinct which naturally makes them interesting and important for the 'weird' tale that according to Lovecraft's famous essay 'Supernatural Horror in Literature' must hold:

> A certain atmosphere of breathless and unexplainable dread of outer, unknown forces (…); and there must be a hint, expressed with a seriousness and portentousness becoming its subject, of that most terrible conception of the human brain – a malign and particular suspension or defeat of those fixed laws of Nature which are our only safeguard against the assaults of chaos and the daemons of unplumbed space.[4]

Lovecraft is undoubtedly best known for his tales of terror and horror, but he kept a close relationship with wonder throughout his life and this even though he lived in an age where wonder, due to the advancement of science, had suffered hyperbole, ridicule and been reduced to a sentiment for the naïve and foolish.

Lovecraft was of a particular sort. He was, as the Germans would say, 'wundersüchtig', meaning roughly that he had an affinity for the supernatural or that which lies just beyond our senses. Lovecraft writes:

4 H. P. Lovecraft, 'Supernatural Horror in Literature', in *Collected Essays, Volume 2: Literary Criticism*, S. T. Joshi, ed. (New York: Hippocampus Press, 2004), 82–135.

> Pleasure to me is wonder – the unexplored, the unexpected, the thing that is hidden and the changeless thing that lurks behind superficial mutability. To trace the remote in the immediate; the eternal in the ephemeral; the past in the present; the infinite in the finite; these things are to me the springs of delight and beauty.[5]

The citation bears witness to Lovecraft's Romanticism and poetical acumen and it is clear that he views wonder as something positive. This positive attitude is repeated somewhat more passionately in a letter to James F. Morton dated 10 February 1923, stating:

> The one great crusade worthy of an enlightened man is that directed against whatever impoverishes imagination, wonder, sensation, dramatic life, and the appreciation of beauty. Nothing else matters.[6]

Lovecraft's inclination towards Romanticism is clear from reading these lines but one element disturbs the flow of things, and it is the phrase 'enlightened man'. On the face of it the phrase, together with the dramatic outburst on what is important in life, that is, the fight against anything that impoverishes imagination, wonder and so forth is an odd coupling. It leaves us to ponder what exactly Lovecraft means by 'enlightened'. What can he possibly have in mind if not the scientific views of the enlightenment period, which as it were stand in opposition to the Romantic thoughts he otherwise advocates? This is a difficult question and cannot be answered in full here, but I am inclined to think that he, like the Romantic poet Percy Shelley, embraced scientific thought as well as the language of the heart in a self-styled rebellion against the wonderless zeitgeist of his age.

5 See H. P. Lovecraft, 'In Defence of Dagon', in *Collected Essays, Volume 5: Philosophy, Autobiography & Miscellany*, S. T. Joshi, ed. (New York: Hippocampus Press, 2006), 53.

6 See H. P. Lovecraft's 10 February 1923, letter James F. Morton in Lovecraft, *Selected Letters I 1911–1924*, 209.

Lovecraft: A Romantically Inclined Wonder-Monger

Terror, it might be ventured, is a state of mind we experience when bodily injury likely to cause death is close at hand, and horror is the state of mind we experience if our lifeworld is suddenly threatened or destroyed. Wonder is more complicated and thus it is a state of mind that has enjoyed many definitions throughout the ages. Plato famously stated in the *Theaetetus* that wonder is the feeling of the philosopher and French philosopher René Descartes believed wonder to be the first of all the passions.[7] As mentioned in the first chapter my own somewhat prosaic definition goes like this: 'Wonder is a sudden experience that intensifies the cognitive focus and awareness of ignorance about a given object.'[8] Adding to the definition one might argue that wonder is typically an unsettling yet delightful experience – and something perhaps we ought to seek out.

Lovecraft certainly sought out wonder, and particularly wonder transmitted through literature, because during his childhood he spent much time reading books of marvels such as *The Arabian Nights*, Hawthorne's *Wonder Book* and *Tanglewood Tales* and the travel literature of Marco Polo and Sir John Mandeville. These sources together with the works of literary thaumaturge Lord Dunsany later inspired Lovecraft to write his own wonder stories – stories that are littered or densely packed with wonder-evoking tropes that play to the imagination producing small sunlit windows in the mind of the reader through which a larger world becomes present.

To bring further insight into how a weird story can be densely packed with wonder let us now explore four types of wonder-evoking tropes that Lovecraft frequently made use of in his fiction.

7 See René Descartes, 'The Passion of the Soul', in *The Philosophical Works of Descartes*, John Cottingham, trans. (Cambridge: Cambridge University Press, 1985), 53.

8 See chapter 1 page 18 & Pedersen, *Balanced Wonder*, 1.

Trope 1: Deliberately Vague and Suggestive Writing

Lovecraft had an affinity for overusing adjectives and if there ever was a master of vagueness and suggestion Lovecraft is truly a worthy candidate for the title. To illustrate this let us focus on a couple of excerpts from his 1925 short story 'The Unnameable':

> It had been an eldritch thing (…). So little is known of what went on beneath the surface – so little, yet such a ghastly festering as it bubbles up putrescently in occasional ghoulish glimpses. (…) And inside that rusted iron straitjacket lurked gibbering hideousness, perversion, and diabolism. Here, truly, was the apotheosis of the unnameable.[9]

Even if one understands every word of the sentences above reading them tends to make the reader feel rather thick-headed because it is hard to pinpoint exactly what Lovecraft is seeking to communicate despite his use of guiding adjectives such as 'eldritch', 'ghastly' and 'ghoulish'. He goes to great lengths to explain just how dire things are but without really revealing what is amiss. Stylistically this is a clever move in a weird tale because it induces wonder in the reader who becomes aware of his or her ignorance concerning the matter at hand. It is also commensurate with Lovecraft's personal outlook on how a weird story is to be crafted. He writes:

> Atmosphere, not action, is the great desideratum of weird fiction. Indeed, all that a wonder story can ever be is *a vivid picture of a certain type of human mood.* The moment it tries to be anything else it becomes cheap, puerile, and unconvincing.[10]

Weird fiction relies on vague and suggestive writing for it to work its wonder and leans heavily on the Baconian idea of wonder as broken knowledge. As a general rule it cannot deal in explanations because explanations are the great neutraliser or the very antidote to wonder. Weird

9 H. P. Lovecraft, 'The Unnameable', in *The New Annotated H. P. Lovecraft*, Leslie S. Klinger, ed. (New York: Liveright Publishing Corporation, 2014), 118.

10 See H. P. Lovecraft, 'Notes on Weird Fiction', in *Collected Essays, Volume 2: Literary Criticism*, S. T. Joshi, ed. (New York: Hippocampus Press, 2004), 177.

fiction, in other words, breaches gaps. The only way an explanation can be used effectively in a wonder story is if it is but a small piece of a larger puzzle of unknown shape or form. Dark corners or unknown regions simply must be present for it to work. (see Figure 5.1).

Figure 5.1. Les Edwards, *The Necronomicon: Sentinel Hill*, 2007. Courtesy of Les Edwards.

Trope 2: Between Worlds

Lovecraft's wonder stories are often escapist in nature. They have a hint of the fanciful and they produce a wondrous atmosphere of mysterious faraway places not unlike the ones we find in the medieval travel literature.

The stories usually revolve around a sensitive poet-like protagonist tired of life's trivialities. The person is ghostlike, alienated, with one foot in our world and the other in what Lovecraft labels the Dreamlands, which is a part of reality accessible only to a sensitive few in Lovecraft's fictional universe. One of these sensitive few is Lovecraft's alter ego Randolph Carter, a character who features in several wonder stories, including 'The Silver Key' (1929), where we find the following peculiar passage:

> When Randolph Carter was thirty he lost the key to the gate of dreams. Prior to that time he had made up for the prosiness of life by nightly excursions to strange and ancient cities beyond space, and lovely, unbelievable garden lands across ethereal seas; but as middle age hardened upon him he felt these liberties slipping away little by little, until at last he was cut off altogether.[11]

The citation reveals a protagonist twice burdened. *Prima facie* Carter is tormented by his prosaic life, which makes him a Lovecraftian pendant to the ennui-hunted Byronesque Romantic or the pleasure-seeking Kierkegaardian *aesthete*. Painful as this may be, he is on top of that distressed about his lost ability to enter the Dreamlands – an extraordinary world he has confirmed the existence of *a posteriori*. Consequently, he stands between worlds not only because such worlds actually exist in Lovecraft's universe but because he has a preference for the world of the Dreamlands now painfully out of reach. Thus, the Dreamlands effectively become a paradise lost – a place of wonder that either like Arcadia is impossible to explore because it is evermore unreachable, or like the utopias of Plato or St Augustine's that, although realisable in theory, seemingly remain out of reach.

The 'between worlds' trope is also used in the Lovecraft's prose poem 'Celephaïs' (1922) where he writes:

> There are not many persons who know what wonders are opened to them in the stories and visions of their youth; for when as children we listen and dream, we think but half-formed thoughts, and when as men we try to remember, we are dulled and prosaic with the poison of life. But some of us awake in the night with strange phantasms of enchanted hills and gardens, of fountains that sing in the sun, of golden cliffs overhanging murmuring seas, of plains that stretch down to sleeping cities of bronze and stone (…) and then we know that we have looked back through the ivory gates into that world of wonder which was ours before we were wise and unhappy.[12]

11 H. P. Lovecraft, 'The Silver Key', in *The New Annotated H. P. Lovecraft*, Leslie S. Klinger, ed. (New York: Liveright Publishing Corporation, 2014), 158.

12 Lovecraft, 'Celephaïs', 72.

In this passage we hear more about the Dreamlands, but we also learn that according to Lovecraft we tend to lose the ability to wonder when we grow up. For some, adulthood equals becoming wise and unhappy, but wise and unhappy are not immediately natural bedfellows. What Lovecraft could have in mind here is the stoic outlook many to some extent adopt in later years. Lovecraft harboured a fierce aversion towards stoicism, mainly because stoicism is against wonderment and portrays the world as disenchanted. The tranquillity of mind that stoicism offers as a path to happiness is rooted in pantheistic metaphysics, claiming that the universe is material and equals one living being that can be addressed as either God or nature. Such a worldview leaves no room for other worlds; and escape, as it were, is impossible – and this Lovecraft could not tolerate. It was simply too bitter a pill to swallow for a Romantic and 'wundersüchtiger' gentleman like himself.

Trope 3: The Lonely Protagonist

Lovecraft's wonder stories also tend to centre on a lonely figure that is waiting or longing for something beyond what normal human life can provide. We find such a character in the opening of Lovecraft's short story 'The White Ship' (1919):

> I am Basil Elton, keeper of the North Point light that my father and grandfather kept before me. Far from the shore stands the grey lighthouse, above sunken slimy rocks that are seen when the tide is low, but unseen when the tide is high. Past that beacon for a century have swept the majestic barques of the seven seas. In the days of my grandfather there were many; in the days of my father not so many; and now there are so few that I sometimes feel strangely alone, as though I were the last man on our planet.[13]

The strange, lonely setting, together with the somewhat contemplative mood of the protagonist, adds to the wondrous and I dare say Romantic atmosphere, because such a character in such a place is both frightening

13 See Lovecraft, 'The White Ship', 70.

and fascinating. Frightening because most of us have a hard time being alone, particularly for prolonged periods. Fascinating because we naturally ask ourselves: how does he endure it? What is his secret?

Trope 4: Mixing Reality and Fiction

In his fictional work Lovecraft deliberately mixes reality and fiction to plant a sense of wonder in the reader. Many of his stories are set in real cities such as Boston, Providence and New York but equally many are set in fictional New England towns such as Arkham, Innsmouth, Dunwhich and Kingsport. Together they form what may be called Lovecraft country, a place where reality and fiction blend together – a place ripe for wonder and wonders.

Blending reality with fiction is not only happening in terms of settings in Lovecraft's work. Many of the scholarly professor-type heroes in Lovecraft stories at some point stumble upon a library extraordinaire, and what makes these libraries special is that some of the books – although old and obscure – are recognisable to the informed reader. James Frazer's *The Golden Bough*, Geber's *Liber Investigationis,* Margaret Murray's *Witch Cult in Western Europe* and Roger Bacon's *Thesaurus Chemicus* are among the titles in question. However, Lovecraft has a habit of casually adding fictional books such as Abdul Alhazred's *Necronomicon*; Ludwig Prinn's *De Vermis Mysteriis* or the *Pnakotic Manuscripts* to the arcane collections. The result is wondrous as the informed reader suddenly feels less informed, bordering on ignorant, because what lore do these books contain, who were their authors and how does one get hold of the books?[14]

14 It must be said that with the Internet at our disposal finding out that these ancient tomes are fictional is relatively easy nowadays. However, when I began reading Lovecraft as a teenager the Internet did not exist and my access to the English-speaking world, including English literature, was rather limited. This resulted in (much to my embarrassment today) years of wondering about the status of Lovecraftian books such as *The Necronomicon*.

Dark Wonder and Dark Romanticism

So much for wonder-evoking tropes. I will close the chapter by addressing the idea of 'dark wonder' and Dark Romanticism in relation to Lovecraft and give reasons why I think Lovecraft's weird fiction can be edifying.

Dark wonder is something that comes up every now and then in the literature on wonder. If we look at the work of psychiatrist Paul Fleichman, we see that he relates the term to the character Ishmael, the fictional narrator in Herman Melville's *Moby Dick*. Here wonder is the salvation for the unshored modern mind because it encompasses violence, cruelty, destruction and annihilation.[15]

Dark wonder also features in Casper Henderson's *A New Map of Wonders* where it is associated with the mental darkness or aporia we experience upon considering the nature of black holes. A black hole emerges when a star much larger than our own sun turns supernova and its core collapses inwards and becomes a singularity – 'a region in space where matter is infinitely dense and space-time infinitely curved'.[16] The monstrous gravitational pull of a black hole allows nothing to escape, not even light, and because of the sheer power of the thing one would think that 'awe' would be the appropriate response. After all, 'awe' is strongly connected with terror, fear and majestic powers beyond our control.[17] However, 'dark wonder' is also quite fitting in relation to black holes because there is much uncertainty surrounding them – an uncertainty that cuts deep into the realm of physics, exposing the division on the nature of black holes between supporters of the theory of general relativity and advocates of quantum theory.

Now I should think it fitting to use the term 'dark wonder' in relation to Lovecraft too, and the reason for that is twofold.[18] Firstly, Lovecraft's

15 See Paul R. Fleischmann, *Wonder: When and Why the World Appears Radiant* (Amherst: Small Batch Books, 2013), 362–363.

16 Caspar Henderson, *A New Map of Wonders: A Journey in Search of Modern Marvels* (London: Granta Publications, 2017), 64.

17 See Pedersen, *Balanced Wonder*, 39.

18 It is possible that Lovecraft himself would have approved of the term because in his 1927 novella *The Dream-quest of Unknown Kadath*, published posthumously by

stories usually end in madness or death. In a traditional hero's journey, a protagonist may go through many trials but at the end of it all he or she will emerge triumphant, and all is well. Lovecraft does not offer that and the typical Lovecraftian protagonist usually finds himself on an endless ghost train ride or in a 'Hotel California situation' where you can check out any time you like, but you can never leave.

Secondly, Lovecraft's cosmic indifference permeates most of his stories and earlier I presented an excerpt from one of Lovecraft's letters to James F. Morton but left out what immediately follows:

> And not even this really matters in the great void. But it is amusing to play a little in the sun before the blind universe dispassionately pulverises us again into that primordial nothingness from whence it moulded us for its second's sport.[19]

The last sentences bear witness to Lovecraft's view of the world as completely indifferent to how our individual lives play out, but coupled with the first two sentences in the earlier quotation a certain defiant Romanticism emerges, celebrating the use of imagination and the significance of the person of feeling and action. In some sense this is life-affirming and quite the antithesis to Michel Houellebecq's famous outlook on Lovecraft portraying the gentleman of Providence as *Contre le Monde, Contre la Vie* or against the world, against life.[20] Thus 'dark wonder' understood in view of Lovecraft's weird fiction, and especially his wonder stories, should not scare us away despite its undercurrent of gloom. It should be studied as it kindles our metaphysical imagination in the wake of a confrontation with a hitherto unknown reality involving mad gods, inter-dimensional beings, human fortitude and perhaps most unsettling of all, human frailty. It should also be studied because it exposes us to a different Lovecraft – a Lovecraft that is wonderfully puzzling if not paradoxical at times.

Arkham House in 1943, he mentions 'dark wonders' in connection to the strange beings inhabiting the dream city of unknown Kadath (Lovecraft 1943).

19 See H. P. Lovecraft's 10 February 1923, letter James F. Morton in Lovecraft, *Selected Letters I 1911–1924*, 209.

20 See Michel Houellebecq, *Against the World, Against Life* (London: Gollancz, 2005).

Now one might attempt a rebuke by interjecting that 'dark wonder' is, but an unnecessary compound word invented, perhaps, to make horror sound nicer and wonder less naïve, or perhaps just to make wonder encompass more of the territory usually affiliated with horror. This may be, but Moby Dick, black holes and Lovecraft's weird fiction hint to us that there is an extraordinary state of mind that is neither horror nor strictly speaking wonder but close to both. 'Awe' seems a worthy candidate for precisely such a state but although fear is clearly present in Lovecraft's fiction awe's other companion, 'terror', is seldom there and thus something is not quite right. Admittedly 'dark wonder' is a somewhat weird label, but it may be easier to digest if one imagines a circle with a fine split in it. At one end is horror, you go around the circle to wonder and on the other end of the circle, close to horror yet not horror, is dark wonder.[21]

Now if dark wonder is indeed a thing and applicable to Lovecraft and his work one might be tempted to group him together with Dark Romantics such as Charles Baudelaire, E. T. A. Hoffmann, Herman Melville and Edgar Allan Poe.[22] However, viewing Lovecraft as a Dark Romantic is problematic and there are at least two reasons for that.

First, Dark Romanticism centres on diabolism, the macabre, the irrational and pessimism when it comes to human life, but such elements can only be found in some of Lovecraft's literary work including short stories such as 'The Tomb' (1922) and 'In the Vault' (1925) and thus Dark Romanticism does not cover the whole of Lovecraft so to speak.

Secondly, Lovecraft's wonder stories exude a certain optimism fuelled by the attention to beauty, the existence of the Dreamlands and the potential for a happy outcome which is sorely absent in Dark Romanticism.

21 The image of the circle with a thin split is borrowed from psychiatrist and early LSD researcher Sidney Cohen who in the 1987 BBC documentary entitled *The Beyond Within—The Rise and Fall of LSD* explained the difference between 'sanity', 'insanity' and 'unsanity'.

22 Dark Romanticism is a literary term thought to originate in the German translation of Mario Praz's 1930 book *La carne, la morte e il diavolo nella letteratura romantica*. The German title of Praz's book is *Liebe, Tod und Teufel: Die schwartze Romantic* which renders into 'Love, Death, and Devil: Dark Romanticism' in English. See Felix Krämer, 'Dark Romanticism: An Approach', in *Dark Romanticism: From Goya to Max Ernst*, Felix Krämer, ed. (Ostfildern: Hatje Cantz Verlag), 15.

Myths and stories are composed of wonders, as Aristotle tells us and when we actively study them, we are in effect exposing ourselves to wonders and indeed the experience of wonder.[23] Reading Lovecraft's weird fiction has the same effect because it is the kind of literature that makes us traffic in cosmology, and engage with fundamental questions about the nature of reality and what is really important for us human beings. The wonders found in Lovecraft works can be edifying partly because they exercise our imagination in an unusual way, making us imaginatively fit and rich in perspective. Naturally, such enrichment does not entail that we take on board his position of cosmic indifference or believe in the existence of, for example, the Dreamlands. Considering them is enough to bring about the edifying and perspective-enriching effect.

Some years ago, I co-taught an elective course labelled 'Existential Themes Through the Prism of Palliation' and during the course my students were working with a prose poem of Lovecraft's entitled 'Ex Oblivione' meaning 'from oblivion'. The poem revolves around a narrator at the end of his life who loves the irradiate refuge of sleep because via sleep he escapes the prosiness of life and enters the Dreamlands where he wanders through old gardens and enchanted woods finding a little of the beauty he had sought in life.

Some of my students were quite touched by the tenderness of Lovecraft and the images his poem conjured up, while others expressed, they felt better prepared for work in palliative care after having read and discussed 'Ex Oblivione' partly because it addresses a taboo namely the tediousness of the commonplace. Although working with poetry such as this was unusual for my students it is my belief that it trained their sensibility and ability to put themselves in another person's shoes. Showcasing sympathy and displaying empathy requires intense work of the imagination and a willingness to engage with wonders. In this regard reading Lovecraft's work offers a great learning opportunity because his weird fiction is a catalyst for wonder precisely because it is loaded with wonder (dark or not) per design.

23 Aristotle, *The Metaphysics*, Hugh Tredennick, trans., Loeb Classical Library (Cambridge, MA: Harvard University Press, 1933), I. II. 10.

Bibliography

Aristotle, *The Metaphysics*, Hugh Tredennick, trans., Loeb Classical Library (Cambridge, MA: Harvard University Press, 1933).

Carson, Rachel, *The Sense of Wonder* (New York: HarperCollins, 1984).

Descartes, René, *The Philosophical Works of* Descartes, John Cottingham, trans. (Cambridge: Cambridge University Press, 1985).

Fleischmann, Paul R., *Wonder: When and Why the World Appears Radiant* (Amherst: Small Batch Books, 2013).

Henderson, Caspar, *A New Map of Wonders: A Journey in Search of Modern Marvels* (London: Granta Publications, 2017).

Houellebecq, Michel, *Against the World, Against Life* (London: Gollancz, 2005).

Krämer, Felix, ed., *Dark Romanticism: From Goya to Max Ernst* (Ostfildern: Hatje Cantz Verlag, 2013).

Lovecraft, H. P., *Collected Essays, Volume 2: Literary Criticism*, S. T. Joshi, ed. (New York: Hippocampus Press, 2004).

Lovecraft, H. P., *Collected Essays, Volume 5: Philosophy, Autobiography & Miscellany*, S. T. Joshi, ed. (New York: Hippocampus Press, 2006).

Lovecraft, H. P., *Eldritch Tales: A Miscellany of the Macabre*, Stephen Jones, ed. (London: Gollancz, 2011).

Lovecraft, H. P., *Selected Letters I 1911–1924*, August Derleth & Donald Wandrei, eds (Sauk City, WI: Arkham House Publishers, 1965).

Lovecraft, H. P., *The New Annotated H. P. Lovecraft: Beyond Arkham*, Leslie S. Klinger, ed. (New York: Liveright Publishing Corporation, 2019).

Lovecraft, H. P., *The New Annotated H. P. Lovecraft*, Leslie S. Klinger, ed. (New York: Liveright Publishing Corporation, 2014).

Pedersen, Jan B. W., *Balanced Wonder: Experiential Sources of Imagination, Virtue, and Human Flourishing* (Lanham: Lexington Books, 2019).

Prinz, Jesse, 'How Wonder Works', *Aeon Magazine* (2013), http://aeon.co/magazine/psychology/why-wonder-is-the-most-human-of-all-emotions/, accessed 2 July 2019.

Tanner, Tony, *The Reign of Wonder: Naivety and Reality in the American Literature* (Cambridge: Cambridge University Press, 1965).

CHAPTER 6

H. P. Lovecraft and the Dunsanian Conjuration

Come with me, ladies and gentlemen

Who are in any wise weary of London:

Come with me: and those that tire at all

of the world we know: for we have new worlds here.[1]

This chapter focusses on Howard Phillips Lovecraft's Romantic sensibilities by paying attention to what the gentleman of Providence, in a somewhat paroxysmic epistle, phrased the 'Dunsanian Conjuration'.

It begins with a brief sketch of Lord Dunsany; the eponym of the phrase and brings to the fore evidence of how Dunsany influenced Lovecraft as a seeker of wonder.

The chapter continues with an exegesis showcasing what the 'Dunsanian Conjuration' is all about, followed by an apology arguing that the Dunsanian Conjuration has an honourable and practical use.

This leads to the conclusion that Lovecraft, as a Dunsanian conjurer par excellence, is no performer of cheap tricks, but a Romantic applying his intellect to cope with a most challenging life, and in doing so, has granted us a tool helpful beyond his own lifeworld – a tool that can be put to good use by contemporary people.

1 See the preface to Lord Dunsany's 'The Book of Wonder', in *Wonder Tales* (New York: Dover Publications, 2003).

The Dunsanian Influence

Edward John Moreton Drax Plunkett, eighteenth baron of Dunsany was born in 1878 at 15 Park Square in London and died quietly, aged 79 in the autumn of 1957, in a nursing home in Dublin following a nocturnal appendectomy from which he never regained consciousness.[2]

Friends and relatives called him Eddie, but his publishing name was Lord Dunsany and with his 6 ft. 4 inches in height,[3] large hands and feet, he cut an impressive figure in his day.[4]

He lived most of his life at Dunsany Castle in county Meath, Ireland, and was a first-rate horseman, hunter and cricketer, and enjoyed boating and cross-country runs as well as chess; the latter to such an extent that in 1942 he invented his own variant of the game labelled 'Dunsany's chess' or simply 'Dunsany's game' (see Figure 6.1).[5]

2 See Mark Amory, *Lord Dunsany: A Biography* (London: Collins, 1972), 13, 282.

3 In a letter to Reinhardt Kleiner dated 9 November 1919, Lovecraft writes that Dunsany was 6 ft. 2 in height, very slender and of a Galpinian build which is a reference to his friend and fellow amateur journalist Alfred Calpin. See Lovecraft, *Selected Letters I 1911–1924*, 91. In the essay 'Lord Dunsany and his work' Lovecraft states that Dunsany is 6 ft. 4 and of medium breath equipped with a fair complexion, blue eyes, high forehead, light brown hair with small moustache to match. See H. P. Lovecraft, *Collected Essays Volume 2: Literary Criticism*, S. T. Joshi, ed. (New York: Hippocampus Press, 2004), 59.

4 See L. Sprague de Camp, *Literary Swordsmen and Sorcerers: The Makers of Heroic Fantasy* (Sauk City, WI: Arkham House Publishers, 1976), 50.

5 See Amory, *Lord Dunsany*, 20, 22 & D. B. Plitchard, *The Encyclopaedia of Chess Variants* (Surrey: Games & Puzzles Publications, 1994), 97. Dunsany chess or Dunsany's game is asymmetrical in the sense that one side has standard pieces while the other is equipped with 32 pawns. Lovecraft did not show much love for chess. He believed it a gentleman's game, but he was not good at it and forgot the rules at least three times. See Lovecraft's letter to James F. Morton dated 23 February 1936, in H. P. Lovecraft, *Selected Letters* V *1934–1937*, August Derleth & James Turner, eds (Sauk City, WI: Arkham House Publishers, 1976).

Figure 6.1. Harry Evans, *Dunsanian,* 2023. Courtesy of Harry Evans.

Lord Dunsany was nearly a teetotaller and only occasionally smoked a respectable pipe, and because he cared little for appearances, he earned the somewhat unflattering label of ' the worst dressed man in Ireland' (see Figure 6.2).[6]

He was well educated and went to Cheam, Eton and later Sandhurst and acquired an intimate understanding of biblical texts, Greek language and mythology.[7] He also became well versed in the works of superlative

6 See Amory, *Lord Dunsany*, 32, 167; Sprague de Camp, *Literary Swordsmen and Sorcerers*, 50 & H. P. Lovecraft, 'Lord Dunsany and His Work', in *Collected Essays Volume 2: Literary Criticism*, S. T. Joshi, ed. (New York: Hippocampus Press, 2004), 59.

7 Cheam or Cheam School is an English private school affiliated with the Anglican church founded in 1645 by George Aldrich and was originally located in a house known as Whitehall in Cheam, Surrey. Today the school occupies four houses: Aldrich, Beck, Gilpin and Tabor and is located in Headley, Hampshire. Eton or Eton College is an exclusive independent boarding school in Eton, close to Windsor in England. It was founded in 1440 by King Henry VI as Kynge's College of Our Ladye of Eton beside Windsore as a sister institution to King's

storytellers such as Brothers Grimm, Hans Christian Andersen and Edgar Allan Poe.

Exposure to the Greek language and ancient Greek culture had a profound effect on the young Dunsany, who, in a 1912 letter to the Irish American writer Frank Harris, writes:

> When I learned Greek at Cheam and heard of other Gods a great pity came over me for those marble people that had become forsaken, and the mood has never quite left me. [...] And then one day imagination came to the rescue and I made unto myself gods, and having made gods I had to make people to worship them and cities for them to live in and kings to rule over them, and then there had to be names for the kings and the cities and great plausible names for the huge rivers that I saw sweeping down through kingdoms by night.[8]

What Dunsany is describing is a perspective-enriching transformation prompted by classical education. Engaging with the Greek language made him not only aware of a language other than English but also aware of another culture and deities now relegated to the category of myth. This prompted a certain mood, a state of mind equivalent to a sense of wonder in the young Dunsany that, although associated with loss, boosted his imagination to the extent that he began his own mythmaking, which later became the foundation of much of his literary output.

College, Cambridge. Medievalist and antiquarian ghost story writer M. R. James who was a contemporary of Lovecraft's and whom Lovecraft admired for his ability to call forth horror from the midst of prosaic daily life was schooled at Eton and later served as provost of both King's College and Eton. See H. P. Lovecraft, 'Supernatural Horror in Literature', 121 & Michael Cox, *M. R. James: An Informal Portrait* (Oxford: Oxford University Press, 1983), 28, 50 & 196. Sandhurst or The Royal Military Academy Sandhurst is a British military academy located in the town of Sandhurst, Berkshire in England.

8 See Amory, *Lord Dunsany*, 16.

Figure 6.2. Edward John Moreton Drax Plunkett, eighteenth Baron Dunsany (1878–1957).

During the Second Boer War (1899–1902) Dunsany fought as a soldier in the battle of Graspan and Modder River and in its wake he began writing wondrous stories, which was the beginning of a lifelong dedication to the art of writing (see Figure 6.3).[9] Dunsany's oeuvre consists of numerous short stories, novels, poems, plays, letters and autobiographical

9 The Second Boar War was fought in Southern Africa between the United Kingdom and the Boars of the Transvaal Republic and the Orange Free States. It culminated in British victory and the collapse of the South African Republic and the Orange Free States. For references to how Dunsany was involved see Ibid., 26–27 and Sprague de Camp, *Literary Swordsmen and Sorcerers*, 52.

work, which earned him an honorary doctorate of Letters from Dublin University in 1939.

In subsequent years the appreciation of Dunsany's literary labours continued to mount and in 1940 he received the accolade of being offered Byron Chair of English Literature in Athens, Greece by the British Council, which he accepted, and in 1950 he was nominated for the Nobel Prize in Literature only to lose to the prominent and highly prolific British philosopher Bertrand Russell.[10]

Figure 6.3. *The Battle of Modder River: View of the Engagement as Seen by the Grenadier Guards from Archibald Forbes, Battles of the Nineteenth Century Vol. VI, The Boer War of 1899–1900*. Cassell and Company Ltd., 1901, 89.

Lovecraft discovered Dunsany in 1919 and attended a lecture of his at the Copley-Plaza ballroom, Boston in October of the same year.[11] The gentleman of Providence found the personality of the king of dreams

10 See Amory, *Lord Dunsany*, 247.

11 See H. P. Lovecraft, 'Lord Dunsany and His Work', 59; Sprague de Camp, *Lovecraft*, 139 & H. P. Lovecraft's letter to Reinhardt Kleiner dated 9 November 1919 in *Selected Letters I 1911–1924*, August Derleth & Donald Wandrei, eds (Sauk City, WI: Arkham House Publishers, 1963), 91–93.

'exceedingly attractive' and generously proclaimed Dunsany's literary significance in many of his own works.[12]

Lovecraft's poem 'To Edward John Moreton Drax Plunkett, Eighteenth Baron Dunsany' published November 1919 in *Tryout* 5, No. 11 is a great example in this respect; not only does it read as one long positive appraisal of Dunsany's work; it also praises the baron as the fairest jewel in Hibernia's crown.[13]

Lovecraft also shared his affection for Dunsany in his private correspondence, and in the letter, he sent to one of his closest friends, the novelist and poet Frank Belknap Long, dated 3 June 1923, is pertinent because it reveals Lovecraft's affinity for Dunsany in ornate terms. Lovecraft writes:

> Dunsany *is myself*, plus an art and cultivation infinitely greater. His cosmic realm is the realm in which I live; his distant emotionless vistas of the beauty of the moonlight on quaint and ancient roofs are the vistas I know and cherish.[14]

Lovecraft's lofty praise of Dunsany is manifold, continuous and found perhaps its ultimate form in his literary essay 'Supernatural Horror in Literature' first published in *The Recluse* in 1927. In here he writes:

> Unexcelled in the sorcery of crystalline singing prose, and supreme in the creation of a gorgeous and languorous world of iridescently exotic vision, is Edward John Moreton Drax Plunkett, Eighteenth Baron Dunsany, whose tales and short plays form an almost unique element in our literature.[15]

12 Hazel Littlefield Smith's 1959 biography of Lord Dunsany is titled: *Lord Dunsany: King of Dreams:* A Personal Portrait.

13 See H. P. Lovecraft, 'To Edward John Moreton Drax Plunkett, Eighteenth Baron Dunsany', in *The Ancient Track: The Complete Poetical Works of H. P. Lovecraft*, S. T. Joshi, ed. (New York: Hippocampus Press, 2013), 66–67. Hibernia is the classical Latin name for Ireland. Lord Dunsany was sent a copy of *Tryout* 5 by Lovecraft's fellow amateur journalist Miss Alice Hamlet who accompanied him to the Dunsany lecture in Boston and Lovecraft's poetry was received favourably by Lord Dunsany who in a letter to Miss Hamlet dated 1 December 1919, wrote that he was grateful to Lovecraft for his 'warm and generous enthusiasm, crystallised in verse' See Sprague de Camp, *Lovecraft*, 141.

14 See Lovecraft, *Selected Letters I 1911–1924*, 234.

15 See Lovecraft, 'Supernatural Horror in Literature', 121.

Dunsany is best known for his collection of short stories published in 1905 under the title of *The Gods of Pegāna* and his 1924 fantasy novel *The King of Elfland's Daughter*, but Lovecraft had high praise for some of his other literary accomplishments like *The Book of Wonder* published in 1912. Lovecraft's poem 'On Reading Lord Dunsany's Book of Wonder' published March 1920 in *Silver Clarion* 3, No. 12 testifies to this effect and reveals most poetically the impact this work had, including how it dispelled some of the loneliness he suffered at the time.[16]

The Book of Wonder is praised again in Lovecraft's 1922 essay 'Lord Dunsany and His Work' where we learn that the gentleman of Providence found that 'its brief fantastic tales [held] a certain humorous doubt of their own solemnity and truth'.[17]

According to biographer L. Sprague de Camp, Lovecraft read Dunsany's *Time and the Gods* in September 1919 and apparently the first paragraph stimulated him as if he had received an electric shock.[18] Alas the truth of this is somewhat uncertain because de Camp does not reference where he got this information, but from Lovecraft's essay 'Lord Dunsany and His Work' we know that Lovecraft cherished this particular collection of short stories because it contains what he labels 'the best Dunsanian forms fully developed'.[19] To Lovecraft, this curious formulation covers the:

> Hellenic sense of conflict and fatality, the magnificently cosmic point of view, the superbly lyrical flow of language, the Oriental splendour of colouring and imagery, the titanic fertility and ingenuity of imagination, the mystical glamour of fabulous lands 'beyond the East' or 'at the edge of the world', and the amazing facility for devising

16 See H. P. Lovecraft, 'On Reading Lord Dunsany's Book of Wonder', in *The Ancient Track: The Complete Poetical Works of H. P. Lovecraft*, S. T. Joshi, ed. (New York: Hippocampus Press, 2013), 70–71. Lovecraft also enjoyed the 1916 companion piece to Dunsany's *The Book of Wonder* called *The Last Book of Wonder*, which was originally published as *Tales of Wonder*. See Amory, *Lord Dunsany*, 283.

17 See H. P. Lovecraft, 'Lord Dunsany and His Work', in *The Ancient Track: The Complete Poetical Works of H. P. Lovecraft*, S. T. Joshi, ed. (New York: Hippocampus Press, 2013), 58.

18 Sprague de Camp, *Lovecraft*, 139.

19 See Lovecraft, 'Lord Dunsany and His Work', 58.

> musical, alluring, and wonder-making proper names, personal and geographical, on classical and Oriental models.[20]

Lovecraft's elaboration can be read not only as testimony to his Romanticism but also as an ideal framework or recipe for his own dream-filled wonder stories including 'Celephaïs' (1922) which bears some resemblance to Dunsany's 'The Coronation of Mr. Thomas Shap' from *The Book of Wonder* and 'The Quest of Iranon' (1935), one of Lovecraft's most exquisite Dunsanian outings.[21]

Apropos dreams and wonder, Lovecraft had a distinct affinity for Dunsany's 1910 collection of short stories called *A Dreamer's Tales.* As he writes:

> It cannot be duplicated or even approached. It is a wonder which has restored to us our childhood's dreams, as far as such things can ever be restored; and that is the most blessed happening which the earth may hold.[22]

The poet from Providence's heartfelt appreciation is clear but so is his longing for the restoration of the bygone days of his childhood, which is a reoccurring theme in his wonder stories, including 'The Silver Key' (1929) and *The Dream-quest of Unknown Kadath* (1943).

Dunsany's impact on Lovecraft was profound and shaped his resulting fiction, but Dunsany also influenced him on a more personal level, and this becomes clear upon considering the 'Dunsanian Conjuration' which we shall turn to now.

20 Ibid.

21 Lovecraft states in the essay 'Lord Dunsany and his Work' that Dunsany's best tales are those conceivable only in purple dream. See H. P. Lovecraft, *Collected Essays 2: Literary Criticism*, S. T. Joshi, ed. (New York: Hippocampus Press, 2004), 58.

22 See Lovecraft, 'Lord Dunsany and His Work', 62.

The Dunsanian Conjuration: An Exposition

On All Fools Day, 1 April 1930, Lovecraft sent a letter to pamphleteer, fellow amateur journalist and original Kalem Club member James Ferdinand Morton. The letter concerned cosmicism, extreme sensitiveness and how to deal with both is written in a jaunty and most uplifting manner equipped with hilarious phrases such as '95-proof pink-snake-evoker' and 'ignominious ostrich-act'.[23]

The letter begins with the curious alliteration: 'Flowing Fountain of Factual Fulgence' only to continue with the following colloquial scene-setter:

> ... Reality is all right enough so far as it goes – I'm not one of those frantic bozos who howl that everything is all wrong and poisonous and so on. The only trouble is *that it doesn't go far enough* for a guy with extreme sensitiveness. The faculty of *interest* is a goddam complex thing. It is perfectly true that mild, conventional, and highly respectable people like the average business or professional man can get enough of a kick out of watching the meaningless routine phaenomena of this pimple on the cosmos to warrant their staying alive – but even with them you can see it wears thin now and then, especially in this latest age of standardisation and decreased variety and adventurousness.[24]

23 The Kalem Club consisted of group of friends Lovecraft met with during his time in New York. For more information see Mara Kirk Hart & S. T. Joshi's, *Lovecraft's New York Circle: The Kalem Club, 1924–1927* (New York: Hippocampus Press, 2006). See also Lovecraft, *Selected Letters III 1929–1931*, 138–141.

24 Curiously some of Lovecraft's letters to Morton opens with an alliteration. In a letter dated 19 October 1929, he begins with: 'Parallel-less, Paramount-point of Petrifica-Pierian Peripateticism' and in another dated 12 December 1929, he writes 'Florecent Finial of Fonetik Filosofy'. See Lovecraft, *Selected Letters III 1929–1931*, 31, 90. In other letters to Morton he begins with dramatic salutations such as: 'Hail, Odovakar, Fellow-Chieftain of the Goths', 'Ave Maxime' and 'Most Sovran Citizen'. See Lovecraft, *Selected Letters I 1911–1924*, 210, 217, 225. Why this is so has alas escaped me thus far. For reference to '... Reality is all right enough so far as it goes ...' see H. P. Lovecraft, *Selected Letters III 1911–1924*, August Derleth & Donald Wandrei, eds (Sauk City, WI: Arkham House Publishers, 1965), 138–139.

In the opening passage Lovecraft reveals that he, a man of extreme sensitivity, is bored with reality and that whatever routine phenomena the average person utilises as a justification for continued living is simply not good enough for him. We also get a glimpse of Lovecraft's cosmicism, with his unflattering description of planet Earth as a 'pimple on the cosmos' and his wonder at himself as a complex creature endowed with the mental capacity of having interests beyond the norm.

With this unusual frame, and framing of himself as a man set apart from the average herd, the question remains if a remedy for this unbearable ennui can be found.

Lovecraft offers three different solutions or 'refuges' as he calls them, and each one rests on the premise that '*All* sensitive men have to call in unreality in some form or other or go mad from ennui' or as he alternatively phrases it towards the end of the letter: '[A] highly organised man can't exist endurably without mental expansion beyond objective reality.'[25]

The refuges he offers are (1) alcohol, (2) religion and (3) The Dunsanian Conjuration, of which the latter, according to Lovecraft, is the only viable way forward. Now before we get into the details of the 'Dunsanian Conjuration' let us dwell briefly on the inadequacies of the first two seen from Lovecraft's point of view.

Beginning with alcohol, moonshine or '95- proof pink-snake-evoker' as he phrases it in the letter, Lovecraft was a passionate teetotaller and he did not shy away from sharing his, often pointed, opinions on what he believed to be the corruptive power of liquor.[26]

Around the time the letter to James Ferdinand Morton was written, he had developed a more nuanced picture of alcohol and knew of its 'positive' effects including how it might serve as relief for the downtrodden and those in pain. Thus, it is not surprising that he acknowledges that alcohol may function as an antidote to boredom, but because he finds the consumption of it to be most unaesthetic in practice and degrading in symbolism, he casts it aside as an unworthy remedy.

25 Ibid., 139, 140.

26 Ibid., 139. For more information Lovecraft's teetotalism see Chapter 3.

Now Lovecraft extends the label moonshine to cover the second refuge; religion, which he describes as a 'churchly hootch of belief in immortality and a benign old gentleman with long whiskers [...] and a cosmic purpose'.[27] He further qualifies that religion is but 'puerile in substance and insulting to the intellect in its outright denial of plain facts and objective probabilities' and amounts to nothing but 'opium for the people'.[28]

Needless to say, Lovecraft did not think much of religion as an effective ward against boredom. In fact, he thought that given our knowledge of nature and how it works, religion or Christianity, which he specifically refers to here, will eventually fade away as an obsolete mythology.[29]

According to the gentleman of Providence, the only way to deal with boredom and the surplus of pain life has to offer is to evoke the 'Dunsanian Conjuration', which he describes as:

> An illusion of *fantastic and indefinite possibility* as shadow'd forth in certain aesthetick interpretations of selected objective phaenomena, time-sequences and cosmical and dimensional speculations. [It is] the consciously artificial manipulation of the theogonist's and myth-maker's privilege in manner of the eighteenth Baron Dunsany ... that is, the deliberate exercise of the human instinct for space, reach, adventure, and cosmic identification through the weaving of fantastic aesthetick impressions *as such,* as *not* as to *supplement*, rather than *contradict*, reality.[30]

27 See Lovecraft, *Selected Letters III 1911–1924*, 139.

28 Ibid., 139, 140. In the letter to Morton Lovecraft mentions Russian revolutionary Vladimir Lenin in connection with the famous phrase 'Religion is opium for the people' and it can be found in Lenin's *Socialism and Religion* from 1905. However, the phrase originates in the work of German philosopher and economist Karl Marx who in the introduction to *A Contribution to the Critique of Hegel's Philosophy of Right* written in December 1843/January 1844 writes: '*Religious* suffering is, at one and the same time, the *expression* of real suffering and a *protest* against real suffering. Religion is the sigh of the oppressed creature, the heart of a heartless world and the soul of soulless conditions. It is the *opium* of the people'. See the introduction to Karl Marx, *A Contribution to the Critique of Hegel's Philosophy of Right*. Retrieved 2 April 2020, from <https://www.marxists.org/archive/marx/works/1843/critique-hpr/intro.htm>.

29 See Lovecraft, *Selected Letters III 1911–1924*, 139.

30 Ibid., 139, 140.

At the core of the Dunsanian Conjuration, we find the embrace of facts in conjunction with the conscious act of creating or diving into a wondrous alternative fictional universe, fully accepting that this universe is not real – that it is nothing more than an illusion. In other words, the 'Dunsanian Conjuration' is informed escapism or a coping strategy extraordinaire, conjoining a taste for the fantastic and the aesthetics of myths with scientific discovery and progress.

It is important to understand two things. First, one must acknowledge that Lovecraft had no intention of deluding himself by putting the 'Dunsanian Conjuration' to use. In fact, he claimed he had to stop dreaming about unknown regions including Antarctica and the Arabian Deserta as soon as such parts of the world were submitted to exploration and their secrets exposed.[31] In this way he resembles many a European medieval or renaissance intellectual who, when Asia was explored, either had to give up believing in fabulous races such as Sciapods (creatures with a single large foot) or Blemmyes (headless people with mouths in their chests and eyes on their shoulders) living in India or relocate such creatures of wonder to regions yet to be explored such as Africa.[32]

31 Arabia Deserta is the Latin name for a particular region in the Arabian Peninsula. The name means abandoned or deserted and dates to the Romans who divided the peninsula into Arabia Deserta (or Arabia magna), Arabia Felix and Arabia Petrae. Arabia Deserta was used by English poet and explorer Charles Montagu Doughty in his famous 1888 *Travels in Arabia Deserta* and remained popular as a geographical label throughout the nineteenth and twentieth century. See also Lovecraft, *Selected Letters III 1911–1924*, 140.

32 See Chapter 1 and Rudolf Wittkower, 'Marvels of the East: A Study in the History of Monsters', Journal of the Warburg and Courtauld Institutes 5 (1942), 197. The Warburg Institute.

Figure 6.4. Harry Evans, *Púca*, 2023. Courtesy of Harry Evans.

Secondly, it is important to realise that Lovecraft could not live on scientific discovery and facts alone. As much as he appreciated science, it hollowed out his world and made his existence an utter bore.[33] To live he had to create unreality – he had to build outwards from the existing facts, as he put it, and create a structure of 'indefinite promise and possibility' (see Figure 6.4).[34] Only by consciously adding a dimension of fancy to the world of facts would he stand a chance against the debilitating boredom and cosmicism that permeated his very being, and that is essentially what the Dunsanian Conjuration is all about. It is in a way an escape route for the sensitive intellectual – a transformative way forward for the brutally honest and insightful (but from a cosmic viewpoint) insignificant Romantic, tormented by tedium.

33 For more information on how scientific explanations do away with wonder see Pedersen, *Balanced Wonder*, 32–34. For information on Lovecraft's somewhat ambiguous approach to natural philosophy or scientific progress see chapters 2 and 5.

34 See Lovecraft, *Selected Letters III 1911–1924*, 140.

The Dunsanian Conjuration: An Apology

In the opening of the chapter, I stated that the Dunsanian Conjuration has an honourable and practical use and indicated that it has value beyond the lifeworld of H. P. Lovecraft.

To justify this point, I shall in the following defend the Dunsanian Conjuration against some of the criticism one might reasonably bring forward against it and afterwards briefly highlight ways in which it can be useful. More concretely I shall begin by addressing two arguments against the Dunsanian Conjuration and then move on to present two arguments in favour of the thaumaturgy so to speak.

The Reality Argument Contra The Dunsanian Conjuration

One may argue that the Dunsanian Conjuration is reprehensible because it is not real and merely consist in an enjoyable layer of fancy relative to the conjurer superimposed upon reality. Now I am sympathetic towards this position but for the criticism fully to work it seems to me that one must have a firm grasp on reality which is not as easy as it sounds. In fact, reality is a problem for us human beings and it is well illustrated in Plato's *The Republic* and more precisely in the allegory of the cave. To the bound and purely forward-facing cave dwellers reality, understood as what they see every day, is but the shadowy reflection of puppets projected on the wall in front of them.[35] We find Plato's idea that the world of the senses, that is, the everyday world around us as presented to us via our senses is but a world of shadows. Consequently, we do not have knowledge about the world in which we live, but merely entertain beliefs about it, and should we wish to gain knowledge about the world, we will have to think in terms of another world – a world beyond the senses.

The problem with reality also comes into focus via seventeenth-century French philosopher Rene Descartes' evil demon, presented in his first

35 See Plato, *The Republic* (London: Penguin Books, 1987), 7, 514.

meditation on what can be called into doubt.[36] To Descartes, the senses are dubious and untrustworthy, and this is expressed most vividly in his thought experiment about the evil demon who, without our knowing, is feeding us a complete illusion about the external world equivalent to what the machines are feeding the unfortunate humans in the 1999 science fiction movie *The Matrix* by the Wachowskis. As with Plato, the message is that we must be sceptical about the world of the senses because we have no way of knowing whether what we sense is real or illusory.[37]

The problem of reality presents itself when we ponder the nature of numbers and moral values, but this time the argument takes on another dimension and shows its potency rather differently. It would be difficult to argue that numbers and moral values are not real, because we use numbers every day as well as engage in debates and often heated arguments about what is valuable and what is not.

However, numbers and values are not real in the sense that they are objects floating about in the universe. We cannot simply go out into the world, collect them and bring them back to a laboratory for further investigation. Numbers and moral values are beyond measure and do not have properties such as weight, height, volume, etc. that physical objects normally have. Furthermore, they do not enter into a causal relationship with other objects in the universe, including themselves, and thus avoid

36 See Rene Descartes, *Meditations on First Philosophy* (Cambridge: Cambridge University Press 1996), 15.

37 Plato's allegory of the cave and Descartes' evil demon are the forerunners to the modern epistemological debate surrounding the brain in a vat problem debated by philosophers such as Gilbert Harman and Hilary Putnam. The central problem is how can it be proven that one is not merely a brain in vat being fed information about the external world by an evil scientist. It is debated who first came up with the idea of brain in a vat. Harman allures to the notion in his book *Thought* from 1973 as do Putnam in his book *Reason, Truth, and History* from 1981. In literary circles Anthony Gilmore's novelette, *The Affair of the Brains* published in *Astounding Stories* in March 1932 has been mentioned as the place of origin, but I should think Lovecraft's novella 'The Whisperer in Darkness' from 1931 a good candidate because in here the poor Vermont folklorist Henry Akeley is but a trapped personality in a cylinder controlled by non-human forces.

our sensory apparatus altogether. At best they are abstractions existing only in our minds.

Now, pondering the nature of numbers and moral values and failing to fully grasp their nature makes not only numbers and moral values strange but our own existence highly uncanny, because as mentioned the subjects in question play a huge role in our daily lives. On top of that, the whole matter is uncanny twice over because the uncanniness we experience when pondering the nature of numbers and moral values intensifies when we contextualise the matter and think in terms of realism and anti-realism/idealism.

In our times, claiming that one is a realist is often viewed as estimable because we are likely to associate being a realist with being grounded, practical and not prone to wonder and fancy. However, to be a realist about numbers and moral values one must take a step beyond the senses because the entities in question do not exist in the physical world, but only in our mind's eye.

By contrast, claiming that one is an anti-realist, or an idealist is likely to be met with suspicion, because many associates being anti-realist/idealist with a certain 'wonderlust', loftiness, impracticality and even intellectual blindness. However, odd entities such as numbers and moral values are relatively easier to deal with for the anti-realist/idealist than for the realist, because numbers and moral values are like everything else for the anti-realist/idealist, namely: constructs in our minds.

Now the weirdness of it all deepens when we realise that our notion of reality relies heavily on our sensory organs and perception. Sensory organs are delicate and can be damaged or suffer defects such as in the case of achromatopsia – a disorder of the retina that allows a person only to see the world in black and white. The takeaway here is that from the fact that person X merely sees the world as black and white it does not follow that the world lacks colour altogether but only that the world for Person X is somewhat 'removed' from reality because a vital sensory organ is compromised.

The feeling may also emerge upon realising that sensory organs can be limited. Consider human hearing compared to that of dogs. Human beings can only hear sounds up to about 20,000 Hz and dogs can hear up to 45,000 Hz.[38] There are aspects of the world that we human beings

38 See H. Heffner, 'Perception of Biologically Meaningful Sounds by Dogs', *The*

qua being human beings do not pick up and dogs qua being dogs do pick up. Comparatively human beings are limited by our creaturehood when it comes to picking up information about the world we are situated in, which is disturbing for the epistemologically inclined because how are we to compensate for this lack of sensory quality?

Adding to the trouble, we face the problem of non-human sensory organs such as those that enable a bat's echolocation or bio-sonar. Philosopher Thomas Nagel argues that bats have consciousness but because the sense organs of a bat are unlike any sense organ that we human beings are equipped with we would never really know what the world looks like for a bat, or what it is like to be one.[39] Consequently, according to Nagel, aspects of the world, including the consciousness of a bat eludes us and we are forced to conclude that our access to the world around us is sharply limited.[40]

Moving into deeper water we must recognise that our perceptions can be troublesome because sometimes we disagree on what is right in front of us. Our perceptions as it were, may differ from one another and this is clear if we look upon 'The Duck-rabbit' – the ambiguous figure made famous in philosopher Ludwig Wittgensteins's *Philosophical Investigations.* Originally the figure appeared in the October 23, 1892, issue of the German humour magazine *Fliegende Blätter* and consists of an image that depicts both a rabbit and a duck (see Figure 6.5). Some people only see the rabbit, others the duck, while others see both but cannot see them at the same time. The duck-rabbit teaches us that our perception of the world is not

---

Journal of the Acoustical Society of America, 58 (1975), 124.

39 See Thomas Nagel, 'What Is It Like to Be a Bat?', *The Philosophical Review* 83, no. 4 (1974), 435–450.

40 Nagel's position has been challenged by philosophers Daniel Dennett and Eric Schwitzgebel who, respectively, argues that the consciousness of a bat is not entirely inaccessible to us and that we human beings do make use of bio-sonar everyday but are not aware of it. For further reading see Daniel Dennett, *Consciousness Explained* (Boston: Little and Brown Company, 1991) and Eric Schwitzgebel & Michael S. Gordon, 'How Well Do We Know Our Own Conscious Experience? The Case of Human Echolocation', Philosophical Topics 28 (2000).

uniform even though the perceived object of interest is quite stable and does not change, and our sensory organs are broadly similar.[41]

Welche Thiere gleichen einander am meisten?

Kaninchen und Ente.

Figure 6.5. *Kaninchen und Ente* (Rabbit and Duck), 1892.

To illustrate this further please permit me to share an anecdote. When I was younger, during a period of approximately six months, I daily experienced what academics today label bereavement hallucinations.[42] I would actually 'see' a dear but alas dead friend of mine whenever I was out and about, which was most extraordinary and bewildering because she was visible to me alone, and back then, as well as today, I am not accustomed to seeing dead people walking.[43] Now the importance here is that extraordinary perceptions such as these prompt us to question the nature of

41 See Ludwig Wittgenstein, *Philosophical Investigations*, 4th edn, G. E. M. Anscombe, trans., P. M. S. Hacker & Joachim Schulte, eds (Oxford: Blackwell, 2009), 204 & Pedersen, *Balanced Wonder*, 19.

42 See M. Ratcliffe, 'Sensed Presence without Sensory Qualities: A Phenomenological Study of Bereavement Hallucinations', *Phenomenology and Cognitive Science* 20 (2021), 601–616.

43 For more information on this wonder-inducing event see Pedersen, *Balanced Wonder*, 117.

direct objects of experience and in what sense a person perceives their surroundings directly.

Considering the Dunsanian Conjuration and 'the criticism from reality' in this light it is obvious that great care must be taken when judging what is real and what is not concerning the world in which we live, including the reality of what is conjured up when the Dunsanian Conjuration is performed.

To determine what is real, one must, as philosopher Hans Fink points out, be able to differentiate between 'dream and reality, fiction and reality, science and reality [and] language and reality'.[44] Confusion about such matters can have terrible consequences for one's wellbeing and may lead not only to intellectual bewilderment but also madness and insanity.

Yet reality is a giddy thing though and as Fink states, a child's nightmare is a real dream and not a dream about a dream or a narrative about a dream. Something is happening to the child while dreaming and 'even a dream about a dream is a real dream about a dream, and not a dream about a dream about a dream'.[45]

In this light a child's nightmare is very much real in the sense that the child is dreaming that something terrible is happening even though the terrible thing happening is not really happening.[46] It is an illusion, but an illusion of experience.

To exemplify let me draw attention to my daughter, who when she was very young, enjoyed watching Ray Harryhausen movies with me until we watched *Clash of the Titans* from 1981. The gorgon Medusa appears towards the end of the film, and the following night she experienced a most alarming dream in which snake-haired Medusa slowly slid into her room with the intention of turning her into stone.

Now a teenager, my daughter still views Medusa with some suspicion because although she is aware that the gorgon appearing in her dream was nothing but a phantasm, she is still somewhat scared of Medusa and who can blame her? After all, in some sense the terrifying creature did come

44 See Hans Fink, 'Om sociale konstruktioners virkelighed', in *Filosofiske udspil* (Aarhus: Philosophia, 2012), 161.

45 Ibid.

46 Ibid.

into her room once and there is every possibility that she could return in the future.

Considering all this the criticism from reality is somewhat weakened because what is real is difficult to determine and thus it seems wise not to outright downplay the reality and effect of the conjuration. Every Dunsanian Conjuration is in a sense a real conjuration and not merely a conjuration about a conjuration or some narrative about a conjuration, because if you, dear reader, were to perform your very own Dunsanian Conjuration it would qualify as an occurrence or a worldly happening, even if it was only happening in your mind.

The Escapism Argument Contra The Dunsanien Conjuration

One may also argue that it is ethically problematic to put the Dunsanian Conjuration into use because it amounts to nothing but escapism. This is an understandable criticism which carries a lot of weight, but escapism is not always bad or morally reprehensible and this is especially true when it comes to something as sophisticated as the Dunsanian Conjuration. One of the most important and redeeming elements of the conjuration is that it is not delusional. The conjurer does not live in a blind fantasy world but is aware that whatever is conjured forth is merely fancy – a pleasurable imaginary layer to the lifeworld of the conjurer that can be put down as easily as it can be called up. The Dunsanian Conjuration may qualify as escapism, but it is not given that it is morally wrong or otherwise damaging and something one ought to shy away from. One of the reasons for this is that the Dunsanian Conjuration does produce something real and if such escapist 'magic' can be used to ward off crippling boredom or offer some relief from an otherwise intolerable prosaic life, is it not to be somewhat celebrated? After all the movement is quite practical and as philologist J. R. R. Tolkien states in his 1939 Andrew Lang Lecture 'On Fairy-Stories':

> Why should a man be scorned if, finding himself in prison, he tries to get out and go home? Or if, when he cannot do so, he thinks and talks about other topics than jailers and prison-walls? The world outside has not become less real because the

> prisoner cannot see it. In using escape in this way the critics have chosen the wrong word, and, what is more, they are confusing, not always by sincere error, the Escape of the Prisoner with the Flight of the Deserter.[47]

Again, it must be stressed that the Dunsanian Conjuration is not delusional and thus it would be difficult to hold that the conjurer is a deserter. The performer of the conjuration is aware of what is going on and does not even escape as such from reality but merely builds on it and by doing so softens the negative impact of reality or set of circumstances that are difficult or perhaps even impossible to change for the conjurer. In this light 'the escapism argument' against The Dunsanian Conjuration loses some of its potency but to further reduce its clout let us move on to address some of the positive aspects of the movement.

The Dead-Man-Working Argument Pro the Dunsanian Conjuration

A positive aspect of the Dunsanian Conjuration is that it can bring much-needed relief to those unfortunate souls finding themselves in dead-man-working situations where corporations or institutions have colonised their lives to such an extent that everyday life consists merely of a bundle of routine phenomena, bereft of variety and adventure.[48] If one is unfortunate enough to live such a life then surely from an ethical viewpoint there is every indication to change it but change is not always easy to bring about. Modern living is complicated, demanding and many keep for want of a better term their 'soul-sucking' jobs simply out of need or

47 See J. R. R. Tolkien, 'On Fairy- Stories', in *The Monsters and the Critics and Other Essays*, Christopher Tolkien, ed. (George Allen & Urwin Publishers, 1983), 148. I am grateful to my brother Lars Bjerggaard Pedersen for pointing me in the direction of Tolkien in this regard. Tolkien was familiar with the works of Lord Dunsany and in a letter addressed to Mr Urwin, dated 16 December 1937, he recognised him alongside author of *Gulliver's Travels* Jonathan Swift as an inventor of names. See J. R. R. Tolkien, *The Letters of J. R. R Tolkien*, Humphrey Carpenter & Christopher Tolkien, eds (George Allen & Urwin Publishers, 1981), 26.

48 The term 'dead man working' is from Carl Cederström and Peter Fleming's 2012 book *Dead Man Working* published by Zero Books.

out of fear – a fear spelling out the possibility that life without that job may be even worse. To contextualise, one can imagine that some people are in a sense trapped in an unwanted job because they have a mortgage or student loan to pay back. Others have family members to care for on top of that and are thus troubled twice over. Regardless money is very much needed and thus some people keep working even though their job is detrimental to themselves and deeply unsatisfying. Now in such a situation where one burns the candle at both ends, I should think the Dunsanian Conjuration quite useful because it brings relief devoid of delusion to the suffering conjurer and enables that person to escape from boredom, and a weary prosaic life, at least for a while. It may even encourage such a person to begin to change his or her life little by little towards something better because Lovecraft does not dictate how one is to perform the conjuration nor what it should contain. Nothing prevents a conjuration to cover elements of 'planning ahead' or strategies for 'personal transformation' because the Dunsanian Conjuration draws on the imagination and as philosopher Mary Warnock argues, using the faculty of imagination allows us to think of things which are not there; it enables us to think about the future and 'makes us feel that there exists an infinity of possibilities'.[49]

The Inspiration Argument Pro the Dunsanian Conjuration

Putting the Dunsanian Conjuration to use may also have a positive effect beyond the immediate solace brought on by the augmented reality or the extension of it. Indulging in Dunsanian conjurations may inspire a person's creativity to such a degree that wonderful works of art follow in its wake. Lovecraft's dreamlands stories are exemplary in this regard because the various protagonists including dreamers extraordinaire Randolph Carter, Kuranes and the unnamed narrator in the prose poem 'Ex Oblivione' are all related to Lovecraft's character, personality, aesthetic preferences, dreams and hopes. The protagonists are not self-inserts-in-full but more Lovecraft 'alter egos' or versions of Lovecraft

49 See Mary Warnock, *The Uses of Philosophy* (Oxford: Blackwell, 1992), 154.

placed in extraordinary settings and equipped with special abilities. They are as it were Lovecraft plus a little extra and a testimony to his imaginary powers as well as his Romanticism. Reading the stories certainly provokes the reader to wonder and contemplate and one of the reasons why this is happening is that the stories all touch on familiar, and I dare say Romantic elements including boredom of or dissociation from 'reality' weaved together with nostalgia and what Lovecraft express as 'the pain of lost things and the maddening need to place again what once had been an awesome and momentous place'.[50] Now if one via a Dunsanian Conjuration should feel inspired to create art and go on to actually produce it and make a livelihood out of it then surely the conjuration has practical and praiseworthy usage beyond the fact that it grants non-delusional escape and the possibility of enjoying a 'new world'.

Summary: A Useful Tool

Lord Dunsany's influence on Lovecraft was considerable and that is amply substantiated not only by Lovecraft's claim that 'Dunsany is myself' but also via Lovecraft's dreamland or wonder stories, including gems such as 'Celephaïs' and 'The Quest of Iranon'.

From the plethora of praise the gentleman of Providence assigned to Dunsany in his essays and letters, his admiration for the Irish writer is clear but labelling the Dunsanian Conjuration after Lord Dunsany is perhaps Lovecraft's greatest accolade to the noble baron. At first look, The Dunsanian Conjuration as an activity may seem suspicious but here at the end of the chapter, it comes across as a marvellous piece of wizardry. Lovecraft, as a Dunsanian conjurer par excellence, was no performer of

50 Lovecraft uses the expression in the novella *The Dream-quest of Unknown Kadath* (1927) that brings together many of Lovecraft's previous dreamland or wonder stories. See H. P. Lovecraft, 'The Dreamquest of Unknown Kadath', H. P. Lovecraft, *The New Annotated H. P. Lovecraft: Beyond Arkham*, Leslie S. Klinger, ed. (New York: Liveright Publishing Corporation, 2019), 329.

cheap tricks, but a Romantic applying his intellect to cope with a life most challenging and his dreamland stories testify to that effect. Understood as a practical tool, the Dunsanian Conjuration is useful even beyond the life-world of the gentleman of Providence because it grants the conjurer escape in the form of being situated in a 'new world' without being delusional and it might potentially also help shape a vision of and consequently help forging a future that does not altogether rely on Dunsanian thaumaturgy or escape to be good. Furthermore it may encourage the making of art which is praiseworthy in and of itself but perhaps especially and practically so if it can be appreciated by artist and aesthetes alike.

Bibliography

Amory, Mark, *Lord Dunsany: A Biography* (London: Collins, 1972).

Cederström, Carl & Fleming, Peter, *Dead Man Working* (Winchester: Zero Books, 2012).

Cox, Michael, *M. R. James: An Informal Portrait* (Oxford: Oxford University Press, 1983).

de Camp, L. Sprague, *Literary Swordsmen and Sorcerers: The Makers of Heroic Fantasy* (Sauk City, WI: Arkham House Publishers, 1976).

de Camp, L. Sprague, *Lovecraft: A Biography* (New York: Doubleday, 1975).

Dennett, Daniel, *Consciousness Explained* (Boston: Little, Brown and Company, 1991).

Descartes, Rene, *Meditations on First Philosophy* (Cambridge: Cambridge University Press, 1996).

Dunsany, Lord, *Wonder Tales* (New York: Dover Publications, 2003).

Fink, Hans, *Filosofiske udspil* (Aarhus: Philosophia, 2012).

Forbes, Archibald, *Battles of the Nineteenth Century, Vol. VL, The Boer War of 1899–1900* (London: Cassell and Company Ltd., 1901).

Hart, Mara Kirk & Joshi, S. T., *Lovecraft's New York Circle: The Kalem Club, 1924–1927* (New York: Hippocampus Press, 2006).

Heffner, H., 'Perception of Biologically Meaningful Sounds by Dogs', *The Journal of the Acoustical Society of America*, 58 (1975), 124.

Lovecraft, H. P., *The Ancient Track: The Complete Poetical Works of H. P. Lovecraft*, S. T. Joshi, ed. (New York: Hippocampus Press, 2013).

Lovecraft, H. P., *Collected Essays Volume 2: Literary Criticism*, S. T. Joshi, ed. (New York: Hippocampus Press, 2004).

Lovecraft, H. P., *The New Annotated H. P. Lovecraft: Beyond Arkham*, Leslie S. Klinger, ed. (New York: Liveright Publishing Corporation, 2019).

Lovecraft, H. P., *Selected Letters I 1911 - 1924*, August Derleth & Donald Wandrei, eds (Sauk City, WI: Arkham House Publishers, 1965).

Lovecraft, H. P., *Selected Letters III 1929 - 1931*, August Derleth & Donald Wandrei, eds (Sauk City, WI: Arkham House Publishers, 1971).

Lovecraft, H. P,. *Selected Letters V* 1934–1937, August Derleth & James Turner, eds (Sauk City, WI: Arkham House Publishers, 1976).

Marx, Karl, *A Contribution to the Critique of Hegel's Philosophy of Right*. Retrieved 2 April 2020 from <https://www.marxists.org/archive/marx/works/1843/critique-hpr/intro.htm>.

Nagel, Thomas, 'What Is It Like to Be a Bat', *The Philosophical Review* 83, no. 4 (1974), 435–450.

Plitchard, D. B., The Encyclopaedia of Chess Variants (Surrey: Games & Puzzles Publications, 1994).

Pedersen, Jan B. W., *Balanced Wonder: Experiential Sources of Imagination, Virtue, and Human Flourishing* (Lanham: Lexington Books, 2019).

Plato, *The Republic* (London: Penguin Books, 1987).

Ratcliffe, M., 'Sensed Presence without Sensory Qualities: A Phenomenological Study of Bereavement Hallucinations', *Phenomenology and Cognitive Science* 20 (2021), 601–616.

Smith, Hazel Littlefield, *Lord Dunsany: King of Dreams; a Personal Portrait* (New York: Exposition Press, 1959).

Schwitzgebel, Eric & Gordon, Michael S., 'How Well Do We Know Our Own Conscious Experience?: The Case of Human Echolocation', Philosophical Topics 28 (2000).

Tolkien, J. R. R., *The Letters of J. R. R Tolkien*, Humphrey Carpenter & Christopher Tolkien, eds (London: George Allen & Unwin Publishers, 1981).

Tolkien, J. R. R., *The Monsters and the Critics and Other Essays*, Christopher Tolkien, ed. (George Allen & Urwin Publishers, 1983).

Warnock, Mary, *The Uses of Philosophy* (Oxford: Blackwell, 1992).

Wittgenstein, Ludwig, *Philosophical Investigations*, 4th edn, G. E. M. Anscombe, trans. and P. M. S. Hacker & Joachim Schulte, eds (Oxford: Blackwell, 2009).

Wittkower, Rudolf, 'Marvels of the East: A Study in the History of Monsters', *Journal of the Warburg and Courtauld Institutes,* Vol. 5 (1942), 159-197.

Afterword

> 'Let us descend into the blind world now,' the poet, who was deathly pale, began; 'I shall go first and you will follow me.'[1]

In *H. P. Lovecraft: Midnight Studies*, through six chapters, I have argued for the idea that Lovecraft at heart was a Romantic. It all began with an exploration of Lovecraft's relationship with wonder and how he sought for poetic knowledge. Chapter 2 exposes Lovecraft's Romanticism via his poem 'Fact and Fancy' and his aversion to the cold light of reason and Chapter 3 not only offers an exploration of Lovecraft's dramatic aversion towards alcohol but also makes us aware that Lovecraft entertained a burgeoning interest in what one may call Romantic political philosophy. Chapter 4 highlights the Romantic sensibilities of the gentleman of Providence via the examination of six themes including 'contemplation', 'joy', 'the dramatic', 'the strange', 'the foreign' and 'the beautiful' and the role they play in his short poem 'A Garden'. Chapter 5 pays special attention to how Lovecraft via his fiction induces wonder or dark wonder even and explores in what capacity one may label Lovecraft a Dark Romantic. Chapter 6, the final chapter addresses Lovecraft's Romantic sensibilities via 'The Dunsanian Conjuration' and argues that it is a practical tool that has usage beyond the lifeworld of H. P. Lovecraft understood as it can provide much-needed respite for the downtrodden and perhaps even help generate a vision of a possible future where the need for conjurations no longer exists or at least is diminished. Furthermore, it showed that the Dunsanian Conjuration may inspire art.

The book portrays a rather different gentleman of Providence than most readers of Lovecraft are used to. It makes him less defined, which is unsatisfying in a way because the undefined is wonder-inducing and when

1 Dante Alighieri, *The Divine Comedy* (London: Everyman's Library, 1995), Inferno canto IV, 13.

something provokes wonder it also makes us aware of our ignorance about the very thing we have in sharp focus. In the opening line of *The Metaphysics* the ancient Greek philosopher Aristotle writes that 'All men naturally desire knowledge' and if this is indeed true all human beings must also naturally shy away from ignorance.[2] Not to know is undesirable but what is one to do when the object of wonder – the thing that one desires knowledge about – is a weird fiction author long departed? Here is the rub because Lovecraft only gives away what he left us in his essays, fiction, letters and poetry and thus the researcher, the investigator, is left in an uncomfortable place full of epistemic worry – and justly so because philosophical, biographical and literary studies are at best uncertain and open for discussion because they rely strongly on interpretation.

Why bother studying Lovecraft if certainty is unattainable one may ask? To such a question I can only answer that what has motivated me is a kind of stubbornness combined with an acknowledgement of the fact that although certainty is hard to obtain a greater understanding is nevertheless achievable.

Is *H. P. Lovecraft: Midnight Studies* successful in producing greater understanding then? I should think so because by uncovering Lovecraft's Romanticism it complicates Lovecraft and makes him more nuanced. When I started out, I, like so many other Lovecraftians, was used to the image of a tall, gaunt-looking Lovecraft orientated towards antiquity and science. To some extent I still enjoy this version of Lovecraft because it mirrors the quintessential hardboiled Lovecraftian investigator compelled to explore any shunned house to exorcise its vampirish basement dweller or confront any would-be Crawford Tillinghast at his private quarters to destroy the infernal machinery he has built. However, the trouble is that Lovecraft was more than that in so many ways. The emaciated features associated with the popular image of Lovecraft are not even representative of his looks throughout his adult life. During his time with his wife Sonia Greene, he unbeknownst to many gained a fair amount of weight – so much in fact that he refused to mount a pair of scales when he went above 193 pounds.

2 See Aristotle, *The Metaphysics*, Hugh Tredennick, trans., Loeb Classical Library (Cambridge, MA: Harvard University Press, 1933), 980 a.

In a letter to Maurice W. Moe dated 15 June 1925, Lovecraft writes: 'You know how fat I was in 1923, and how bitterly I resented the circumstance. In 1924 I grew even worse, till finally I had to adopt a # 16 collar.'[3] To be fair, his corpulence did not last for long because after reaching the 16 collar mark Lovecraft, much to the distress of his wife, his aunts and indeed the wife of Frank Belknap Long, dieted himself down to 146 pounds and a collar size of' 14 ¾.[4] When I disclose this bit of information to weird fiction aficionados or Lovecraft buffs an atmosphere of disbelief and scepticism ever so often emerges because the idea of a plump Lovecraft is for many simply absurd and iconoclastic. That Lovecraft at heart was a Romantic is but another element that obfuscates the popular image of Lovecraft and have us realise that the gentleman of Providence is not so easily pigeonholed.

To conclude the book, I should like to say that there is still much to learn about H. P. Lovecraft and that it is my sincere hope that the exploration of his character, persona and life's work in all its guises will continue. Personally, I am eager to learn more about the gentleman of Providence and it does not trouble me in the slightest to admit that even now, after years of study, I still do not consider myself an expert on the man. As Francisco de Goya would say: Aún aprendo.

3 See Lovecraft, *Selected Letters II 1925–1929*, 18.

4 Ibid., 19.

Bibliography

Adelman, Richard, *Idleness, Contemplation, and the Aesthetic, 1750–1830* (Cambridge: Cambridge University Press, 2011).

Alighieri, Dante, *The Divine Comedy* (London: Everyman's Library, 1995), Inferno canto IV, 13.

Amory, Mark, *Lord Dunsany: A Biography* (London: Collins, 1972).

Aristotle, *Metaphysics*, Hugh Tredennick, trans., Loeb Classical Library (Cambridge, MA: Harvard University Press, 1933).

Aristotle, *The Nicomachean Ethics*, H. Rackham, trans., Loeb Classical Library (Cambridge, MA: Harvard University Press, 2003).

Attfield, Robin, *Wonder, Value and God* (London: Routledge, 2017).

Benson-Gyles, Dick, *The Boy in the Mask: The Hidden World of Lawrence of Arabia* (Dublin: The Lilliput Press, 2016).

Berlin, Isaiah, *The Roots of Romanticism*, Henry Hardy, ed. (Princeton, NJ: Princeton University Press, 2001).

Brewer, Keagan, *Wonder and Skepticism in the Middle Ages* (London: Routledge, 2016).

Byron, Lord, *The Complete Poetical Works*, vol. III, Jerome J. McGann, ed. (Oxford: Clarendon Press, 1980).

Byron, Lord George Gordon, *The Works of Lord Byron* (London: John Murray, 1833).

Cannon, Peter, ed., *Lovecraft Remembered* (Sauk City, WI: Arkham House Publishers, 1998).

Card, Jeb J., *Spooky Archaeology* (Albuquerque: University of New Mexico Press, 2019).

Carson, Rachel, *The Sense of Wonder* (New York: HarperCollins, 1984).

Cartmill, Matt, *A View to a Death in the Morning: Hunting and Nature through History* (Cambridge, MA: Harvard University Press, 1996).

Cederström, Carl & Fleming, Peter, *Dead Man Working* (Winchester: Zero Books, 2012).

The Charleston Observer, 10, no. 44 (29 October 1836), 174, Columns 4–5.

Cisco, Michael, *Weird Fiction: A Genre Study* (London: Palgrave Macmillan, 2021).

Cox, Michael, *M. R. James: An Informal Portrait* (Oxford: Oxford University Press, 1983).

Daston, Lorraine & Park, Katharine, *Wonders and the Order of Nature* (New York: Zone Books, 1998).

de Camp, L. Sprague, *Literary Swordsmen and Sorcerers: The Makers of Heroic Fantasy* (Sauk City, WI: Arkham House Publishers, 1976).

de Camp, L. Sprague, *Lovecraft: A Biography* (New York: Doubleday, 1975).

de Deulin, Nathalie de Harlez, 'The Influence of England on the First English Gardens in the Southern Low Countries and the Principality of Liege', in *Garden History*, vol. 44, supplement 44 (Autumn 2016): *Capability Brown: Perception and Response in Global Context: The Proceedings of an ICOMUS-UK Conference held at the University of Bath*, 7–9 September 2016 (Autumn 2016).

Dennett, Daniel, *Consciousness Explained* (Boston: Little, Brown and Company, 1991).

Derie, Bobby, *Sex and the Cthulhu Mythos* (New York: Hippocampus Press, 2014).

Descartes, Rene, Meditations on First Philosophy (Cambridge: Cambridge University Press, 1996).

Descartes, Rene, *The Philosophical Works of Descartes*, vol. 1, John Cottingham, trans. (Cambridge: Cambridge University Press, 1985).

Dunsany, Lord, *Wonder Tales* (New York: Dover Publications, 2003).

Eco, Umberto, *On Beauty: A History of a Western Idea* (London: Secker & Warburg, 2004).

Fink, Hans, *Filosofiske udspil* (Aarhus: Philosophia, 2012).

Finn, Mark, *Blood and Thunder* (Austin: MonkeyBrain Books, 2006).

Fleischmann, Paul R., *Wonder: When and Why the World Appears Radiant* (Amherst: Small Batch Books, 2013).

Forbes, Archibald, *Battles of the Nineteenth Century, Vol. VL, The Boer War of 1899–1900* (London: Cassell and Company Ltd., 1901).

Gately, Iain, *Drink a Cultural History of Alcohol* (Sheridan, WY: Gotham Books, 2018).

Gonzalez, Antonio Alcala & Sederholm, Carl H., eds, *Lovecraft in the 21st Century: Dead, But Still Dreaming* (New York: Routledge, 2022).

Gough, John Bartholomew, *Sunlight and Shadow or Learnings from My Life-Work* (London: Hodder and Stoughton, 1880).

Harman, Graham, *Weird Realism: Lovecraft and Philosophy* (Winchester: Zero Books, 2012).

Hart, Mara Kirk & Joshi, S. T., *Lovecraft's New York Circle: The Kalem Club, 1924–1927* (New York: Hippocampus Press, 2006).

Heffner, H., 'Perception of Biologically Meaningful Sounds by Dogs', *The Journal of the Acoustical Society of America*, 58 (1975), 124.

Henderson, Caspar, *A New Map of Wonders: A Journey in Search of Modern Marvels* (London: Granta Publications, 2017).

Hesiod, *Theogony, Works and Days, Testimonia*, Glenn W. Most, ed. & trans., Loeb Classical Library (Cambridge, MA: Harvard University Press, 1989).

The Holy Bible, King James Version (London: Tophi Books, 1994).

Horace, *Odes and Epodes*, Niall Rudd, trans., Loeb Classical Library (Cambridge, MA: Harvard University Press, 2004).

Horace, *Satires, Epistles, Ars Poetica*, H. R. Fairclough, trans., Loeb Classical Library (Cambridge, MA: Harvard University Press, 1955).

Houellebecq, Michel, *Against the World, Against Life* (London: Gollancz, 2005).

James, M. R. *Collected Ghost Stories*, Darryl Jones, ed. (Oxford: Oxford University Press, 2011).

Joshi, S. T., ed., *H. P. Lovecraft: Four Decades of Criticism* (Athens: Ohio University Press, 1980).

Joshi, S. T., *I Am Providence: The Life and Times of H. P. Lovecraft*, vol. 1 (New York: Hippocampus Press, 2010).

Joshi, S. T., ed., *Lovecraft Annual No. 11* (New York: Hippocampus Press, 2017).

Joshi, S. T., ed., *Lovecraft Annual No. 12* (New York: Hippocampus Press, 2018).

Joshi, S. T., ed., *Lovecraft Annual No. 13* (New York: Hippocampus Press, 2019).

Joshi, S. T., ed., *Lovecraft Annual No. 16* (New York: Hippocampus Press, 2022).

Joshi, S. T., ed., *Lovecraft Annual No. 5* (New York: Hippocampus Press, 2011).

Joshi, S. T., ed., *Lovecraft Annual No. 5* (New York: Hippocampus Press, 2011).

Joshi, S. T., ed., *Lovecraft Annual No. 16* (New York: Hippocampus Press, 2022).

Joshi, S. T., *Lovecraft's Library: A Catalogue*, 3rd edn (New York: Hippocampus Press, 2012).

Joshi, S. T., *Primal Sources: Essays on H. P. Lovecraft* (New York: Hippocampus Press, 2003).

Joshi, S. T. & Schultz, David E., *An H. P. Lovecraft Encyclopedia* (New York: Hippocampus Press, 2001).

Jürgensen, Martin Wangsgaard, *Skrækvisioner* (Odense: Syddansk Universitetsforlag, 2020).

Kant, Immanuel, *Critique of Judgement*, W. S. Pluhar, trans. (Cambridge: Hackett Publishing, 1987).

Keats, John, *The Complete Poems of John Keats*, John Barnard, ed. (London: Penguin Books, 1988).

Keats, John, *The Complete Poetry and Selected Prose of John Keats*, Harold E. Briggs, ed., (New York: Random House, 1951).

Krämer, Felix, ed., *Dark Romanticism: From Goya to Max Ernst* (Ostfildern: Hatje Cantz Verlag, 2013).

Lloyd, Genevieve, *Reclaiming Wonder after the Sublime* (Edinburgh: Edinburgh University Press, 2018).

Locke, John, *Two Treatises of Government*, Peter Laslett, ed. (Cambridge: Cambridge University Press, 1999).

Long, Frank Belknap, *Howard Phillips Lovecraft: Dreamer on the Nightside* (Sauk City, WI: Arkham House Publishers, 1975).

Lord, Evelyn, *The Hell-Fire Clubs: Sex, Satanism and Secret Societies* (New Haven, CT: Yale University Press, 2008).

Lovecraft, *H. P., Collected Essays Volume 1: Amateur Journalism*, S. T. Joshi, ed. (New York: Hippocampus Press, 2004).

Lovecraft, H. P., *Collected Essays Volume 2: Literary Criticism*, S. T. Joshi, ed. (New York: Hippocampus Press, 2004).

Lovecraft, H. P., *Collected Essays Volume 3: Science*, S. T. Joshi, ed. (New York: Hippocampus Press, 2005).

Lovecraft, H. P., *Collected Essays Volume 4: Travel*, S. T. Joshi, ed. (New York: Hippocampus Press, 2005).

Lovecraft, H. P., *Collected Essays Volume 5: Philosophy, Autobiography & Miscellany*, S. T. Joshi, ed. (New York: Hippocampus Press, 2006).

Lovecraft, H. P., *Eldritch Tales: A Miscellany of the Macabre*, Stephen Jones, ed. (London: Gollancz, 2011).

Lovecraft, H. P., 'Old Bugs', *The H. P. Lovecraft Archive*, <http://www.hplovecraft.com/writings/texts/fiction/ob.aspx>

Lovecraft, H. P., *Selected Letters I 1911–1924*, August Derleth & Donald Wandrei, eds (Sauk City, WI: Arkham House Publishers, 1965).

Lovecraft, H. P., *Selected Letters II 1925–1929*, August Derleth & Donald Wandrei, eds (Sauk City, WI: Arkham House Publishers, 1968).

Lovecraft, H. P., *Selected Letters III 1929–1931*, August Derleth & Donald Wandrei, eds (Sauk City, WI: Arkham House Publishers, 1971).

Lovecraft, H. P., *Selected Letters IV 1932–1934*, August Derleth & James Turner, eds (Sauk City, WI: Arkham House Publishers, 1976).

Lovecraft, H. P., *Selected Letters V 1934–1937*, August Derleth & James Turner, eds (Sauk City, WI: Arkham House Publishers, 1976).

Lovecraft, H. P., 'Sweet Ermengarde or the Heart of a Country Girl', *The H. P. Lovecraft Archive*, <http://www.hplovecraft.com/writings/texts/fiction/se.aspx>

Lovecraft, H. P., *The Ancient Track: The Complete Poetical Works of H. P. Lovecraft*, S. T. Joshi, ed. (New York: Hippocampus Press, 2013).

Lovecraft, H. P., *The Annotated H. P. Lovecraft*, Leslie S. Klinger, ed. (New York: Liveright Publishing Corporation, 2014).

Lovecraft, H. P., *The New Annotated H. P. Lovecraft: Beyond Arkham*, Leslie S. Klinger, ed., (New York: Liveright Publishing Corporation, 2019).

Lovecraft, H. P., *The Spirit of Revision: Lovecraft's Letters to Zealia Brown Reed Bishop*, Sean Branney & Andrew Leman, eds (Clendale, CA: HPLHS, 2015).

Lovecraft, H. P., *Tilfældet Charles Dexter Ward* (Århus: Schønberg, 1991).

MacCarthy, Fiona, *Byron: Life and Legend* (New York: Farrar, Straus and Giroux, 2002), 164.

MacCoun, Robert J. & Reuter, P., Drug War Heresies: Learning from Other Vices, Times, and Places (Cambridge: Cambridge University Press, 2001).

Machiavelli, Niccolò, *The Prince*, W. K. Marriot, trans. (Project Gutenberg, 1998).

Marx, Karl, *A Contribution to the Critique of Hegel's Philosophy of Right*. Retrieved 2 April 2020 from <https://www.marxists.org/archive/marx/works/1843/critique-hpr/intro.htm>.

Mieves, Christian & Brown, Irene, eds, *Wonder in Contemporary Artistic Practice* (London: Routledge, 2017).

Mill, John Stuart, *On Liberty* (London: Everyman, 1999).

Monk, Ray, *Bertrand Russell: The Spirit of Solitude* (London: Jonathan Cape, 1996).

Moreland, Sean, ed., *New Directions in Supernatural Horror Literature* (London: Palgrave Macmillan, 2018).

Murray, Christopher John, ed., *Encyclopedia of the Romantic Era: 1760–1850*, vol. 1 (New York: Routledge, 2003).

Nagel, Thomas, 'What Is It Like to Be a Bat', *The Philosophical Review* 83, no. 4 (1974), 435–450.

Nietzsche, Friedrich, *Afgudernes ragnarok*, Jens Erik Kristensen & Lars- Henrik Schmidt, trans. (Copenhagen: Gyldendal, 1999).

Nietzsche, Friedrich, *Beyond Good and Evil*, Walter Kaufmann, trans. (New York: Vintage Books, 1989).

Onians, John, ed., *Sight and Insight: Essays on Art and Culture in Honour of E. H. Combrich at 85* (London: Phaidon Press, 1994).

Pedersen, Jan B. W., *Balanced Wonder: Experiential Sources of Imagination, Virtue, and Human Flourishing* (Lanham, MD: Lexington Books, 2019).

Plato, *The Republic* (London: Penguin Books, 1987).

Plato, *Theaetetus*, H. N. Fowler, trans., Loeb Classical Library (Cambridge, MA: Harvard University Press, 1989).

Platon, *Platon I: Samlede værker i ny oversættelse*, Jørgen Mejer & Chr. Gorm Tortzen, eds (Copenhagen: Gyldendal, 2009).

Platon, *Platon II: Samlede værker i ny oversættelse*, Jørgen Mejer & Chr. Gorm Tortzen, eds (Copenhagen: Gyldendal, 2010).

Plitchard, D. B., The Encyclopaedia of Chess Variants (Surrey: Games & Puzzles Publications, 1994).

Poe, Edgar Allan, *The Complete Poetry of Edgar Allan Poe* (New York: Signet, 2008).

Poe, Edgar Allan, *The Portable Poe*, Philip van Doren Stern, ed. (New York: Penguin Books, 1977).

Polo, Marco, *The Travels*, Nigel Cliff, trans. (London: Penguin Books, 2015).

Pope, Alexander, *The Poetic Works of Alexander Pope*, A. W. Ward, ed. (London: Macmillan, 1885).

Prinz, Jesse, 'How Wonder Works', *Aeon Magazine* (2013), http://aeon.co/magazine/psychology/why-wonder-is-the-most-human-of-all-emotions/, accessed 2 July 2019.

Quinn, Dennis, *Iris Exiled: A Synoptic History of Wonder* (Lanham: University Press of America, 2002).

Racine, Catherine A., *Beyond Clinical Dehumanisation towards the Other in Community Mental Health Care: Levinas, Wonder and Autoethnography* (London: Routledge, 2021).

Ratcliffe, M., 'Sensed Presence without Sensory Qualities: A Phenomenological Study of Bereavement Hallucinations', *Phenomenology and Cognitive Science* 20 (2021), 601–616.

Rorabaugh, W. J., *Prohibition: A Concise History* (Oxford: Oxford University Press, 2018).

Rousseau, Jean-Jacques, *The Social Contract* (London : Penguin Books, 1968).

Russell, Bertrand, *History of Western Philosophy* (London: Routledge, 2009).

Schinkel, Anders, *Wonder and Education: On the Educational Importance of Contemplative Wonder* (London: Bloomsbury Academic, 2021).

Schmitt Carl, *Political Romanticism*, Guy Oakes, trans. (Cambridge, MA: MIT Press, 2011).

Schwitzgebel, Eric & Gordon, Michael S., 'How Well Do We Know Our Own Conscious Experience?: The Case of Human Echolocation', *Philosophical Topics* 28 (2000), 235-246.

Seneca, *Epistles 1–65*, Richard M. Cummere, trans., Loeb Classical Library (Cambridge, MA: Harvard University Press, 1917).

Seneca, *Moral Essays*, vol. II, John W. Basore, trans., Loeb Classical Library (Cambridge, MA: Harvard University Press, 1933).

Shakespeare, William, 'Othello', in *Tragedies*, vol. 1, Sylvan Barnet ed., (London: Everyman's Library, 1992).

Shelley, Mary, *Frankenstein or, The Modern Prometheus* (London: Collectors Library, 2004).

Simmons, David, ed., *New Critical Essays on H. P. Lovecraft* (New York: Palgrave Macmillan, 2013).

Smith, Hazel Littlefield, Lord Dunsany: King of Dreams; a Personal Portrait (New York: Exposition Press, 1959).

Smith, Philip, 'Re-visioning Romantic-Era Gothicism: An Introduction to Key Works and Themes in the Study of H. P. Lovecraft', *Literature Compass* 8/11 (2021), 830–839.

Tanner, Tony, *The Reign of Wonder: Naivety and Reality in the American Literature* (Cambridge: Cambridge University Press, 1965).

Taylor, James S., *Poetic Knowledge: The Recovery of Education* (New York: State University of New York Press, 1998).

Thacker, Eugene, *After Life* (Chicago: The University of Chicago Press, 2010).

Thacker, Eugene, *Horror of Philosophy*, vols 1–3 (Winchester: Zero Books, 2010/ 2015).

The Travels of Sir John Mandeville, C. W. R. D. Moseley, trans. (London: Penguin Books, 1983).

Thomson, Carl, *The Suffering Traveller, and the Romantic Imagination* (Oxford: Clarendon Press, 2007).

Tolkien, J. R. R., *The Letters of J. R. R Tolkien*, Humphrey Carpenter & Christopher Tolkien, eds (London: George Allen & Unwin Publishers, 1981).

Tolkien, J. R. R., The Monsters and the Critics and Other Essays, Christopher Tolkien, ed. (George Allen & Urwin Publishers, 1983).

Trotter, Thomas, *An Essay, Medical, Philosophical, and Chemical on Drunkenness and It's Effect on the Human Body* (London: Printed for T. N. Longman, and O. Rees, 1804).

Vasalou, Sophia, *Wonder a Grammar* (New York: Suny Press, 2015).

Warnock, Mary, *Imagination* (London: Faber & Faber, 1976).

Warnock, Mary, *The Uses of Philosophy* (Oxford: Blackwell, 1992).

Wittgenstein, Ludwig, Philosophical Investigations, 4th edn, G. E. M. Anscombe, trans. and P. M. S. Hacker & Joachim Schulte, eds (Oxford: Blackwell, 2009).

Wittkower, Rudolf, 'Marvels of the East: A Study in the History of Monsters', *Journal of the Warburg and Courtauld Institutes,* Vol. 5 (1942), 159-197.

Wordsworth, William, *The Major Works* (Oxford: Oxford University Press, 2011).

Wordsworth, William, *William Wordsworth: The Major Works*, Stephen Gill, ed. (Oxford: Oxford University Press, 2008).

Index

www.ingramcontent.com/pod-product-compliance
Lightning Source LLC
Chambersburg PA
CBHW070628310726
48982CB00001B/206